5.5

"Irony of Medicine : fuelled by coffee, advising a healthy life"

DR. JAISING VERMA   DR. AADARSH SHIVUM

5. 5

Copyright © 2025 Dr. Jaising Verma and Dr. Aadarsh Shivum. No part of this book may be reproduced or transmitted in any form or by any means, electronic or mechanical including photocopying and recording, by any information storage and retrieval system, without permission in writing from the author. This is a work of fiction. Names, places, characters and incidents are either the product of the author's imagination or are used fictionally for better understanding, and any resemblance to any actual persons, living or dead, organisations, events or locales is entirely coincidental. The details in the book are mere according to the author's understanding, the original concept may differ.

For more information,

Email: jaisingverma@gmail.com
draadarsh910@gmail.com.

Instagram – jv_1997, dr_aadarsh9

Cover – Parth B. Vakharia

Email : artistparthconnect@gmail.com

Instagram - @guy.who.pens

PREFACE

Speaking of medical life in India, to become a doctor, you have to spend countless sleepless nights studying and surviving on caffeine. Then once you get the privilege of putting the prefix 'Dr.' in front of your name, you advise your patients to get a good eight hours of sleep, as it is good for their health and recovery. No wonder medicine was discovered by Hippocrates. That being said, 5.5 years of MBBS were the best time of my life, and what a rollercoaster ride it was. This book is a journey into the heart of one of the most diverse and dynamic healthcare systems in the world.

Dr. Jaising Verma   **Dr. Aadarsh Shivum**

ACKNOWLEDGEMENTS

Hi everyone, we can't possibly thank everyone who has contributed to this book. Every person who ever came into our lives during our MBBS journey has played a part in shaping this book. You all know who you are, and we thank you for the content. We would like to begin with our parents by thanking them for supporting us through every trial. A very special thanks to our editor Dr. Saurbhi, thankyou for being a brilliant editor and a steadfast cheerleader. We are blessed with some amazing friends who supported us throughout - Dr. Zerifa, Dr. Sonali and Ridhi. A heartfelt thank you to Parth, our cover designer, for your incredible creativity and vision in bringing this cover to life. Parth is a visual artist and designer with a background in animation and storytelling. The journey of 5.5 started back in 2023 when we got to know each other and shared our common interest in penning down our MBBS journey. Through this book, we are not trying to portray the most ideal version, like the movies which inspire you to pursue medicine as a career. Instead, our intention is to show you the reality of medicine in the rawest and most wholesome way possible. Hope you enjoy the read.

Dr. Jaising Verma   **Dr. Aadarsh Shivum**

CONTENTS

Page No.

To all the healthcare workers out there, more power to you. You all are doing a great job.

CHAPTER 1

THRESHOLD OF CHANGE

6th May, 2022 was the day of our graduation ceremony. Five and a half years of medical school finally got us here, dressed in formals, in our graduation gowns with the back displaying 'Batch of 2017' in bright gold. Contrary to the unkempt hair, dark circles and poor body odour from the regular night shifts and overtime at the hospital, everyone looked phenomenal in their squeaky-clean new shoes and outfits – as if fresh out of the oven of med school. Everyone was dressed up for tonight. Everyone looked like...a Doctor!

As I entered the auditorium, I saw Natasha. She was waiting near the main stage, picking the exact spot so she

5. 5

could get a full view of the entire auditorium. I was running late as usual, and as always she'd be annoyed at me. I noticed Vivaan and Zeeshan, my colleagues and dear friends, seated two rows ahead of us. Watching them in that moment suddenly took me back in time to my first year. I remember I had already wishlisted outfits for this day years ago. However, as time passed, our friendship weakened over the years and so did my desire for those wishlisted items.As the convocation speeches commenced, the familiar surroundings of the auditorium evoked memories. It was right here that I first heard from Dr. Dhawan, whose guidance and support had been instrumental, especially over the past two years. I tried to catch a glimpse of him sitting in the first row, and as always, he was dressed in his long black coat, blue striped tie and Oxford shoes.

Oh, to hell with the present where everyone is about to separate. Let's go back to the past, where we all first met each other.

5. 5

It was the first day of college. My parents came to drop me
from Pune. They started giving me advice: not to keep any
secrets, to study hard, to make good friends, and to show
respect to my teachers and seniors. But at that moment, I
was in such a nervous blend of anticipation and
excitement that I could barely pay attention to them. I
assumed any cab crossing me with a young boy and
luggage, was heading the same way I was.

I reached college and collected my hostel allotment letter
upon arriving at the administration block. Two people
were assigned to a single room. After a brief walk around
the campus, my parents and I headed to the hostel. To my
disappointment, the accommodation did not look
remotely as close to what our prospectus showed us. It
took me a minute to realise that the images shown in the
prospectus were actually of the new girls' hostel, built with
elevators, gardens and a library on each floor. The hostel
allotted to me looked like a central British Jail with cracks
in the walls and uneven colouring due to weathering and
damage. At the entrance, I noticed three men smoking

cigarettes and being greeted by passing students. I figured they must be seniors, but I hesitated to admit it on my first day, not wanting to concern my parents. As I passed them by, our eyes met and they gave an intense gaze; I immediately shifted my attention.

Upon entering the hostel, we encountered a middle-aged man in the guard's room who greeted my parents with a gesture of *Namaste*. I inquired about the location of Room A-120. He mentioned that my roommate had already arrived earlier in the morning. Juggling two bags, I anxiously glanced back at my parents as we traversed the hostel. The scene was not what they expected— beer cans scattered, looking like remnants of the previous night's party. The walls had broken fixtures, balloon marks and smudged paint. Mum looked disturbed, but my dad asserted proudly that I wouldn't engage in such activities.

As we entered my room, we found one bed already occupied, so I headed to the other side. I unloaded my bags and made space for my parents. Mum promptly scrutinised and criticised the room. Suddenly, it dawned upon me that henceforth I would be on my own. Mum had been holding my hand in the cab throughout the ride to the college. I could have cried, but to cry when people already expect you to cry makes you conscious of your choices. So I headed outside the room saying that I would be back after a short tour of the hostel. Mum followed me out of the room. She wanted to hand me some more money — the kind of transaction your father never finds out about.

The atmosphere was chaotic, with people enjoying themselves, drinking beer and smoking cigarettes. Insects were buzzing around the dustbin, and the walls were covered with graffiti that read 'I challenge you to survive 5 years without Diazepam'. The common room space was cluttered with trash, and leftover food and drink containers, giving the atmosphere a general sense of fatigue. Some seniors were screaming at a junior, asking him to fill a water bottle. Wait! Not just fill it directly under a tap. He was supposed to fill the entire bottle using only the tiny bottle cap. After witnessing this scene, I was terrified. Suddenly I noticed my mum standing behind me. She was even worse; she was petrified! So, I tried to console her, saying, 'Don't worry so much Mum. Arjun bhaiya also stayed in this hostel; he taught me everything. Don't stress, I will manage.' It was time for my parents to leave, and the tears that were mandated to be hidden now called for mutiny. My father who had abstained from showcasing his love for me publicly for eternity, gently tapped my cheeks and wished me luck with tears in his eyes. I decided not to follow them to the cab as it would make me more emotional. I needed to calm myself down before my roommate returned to the room. I wanted him to think that his roommate was more practical and wiser than him. I didn't want to show my vulnerability on my very first night.

I managed to meet a lot of my batchmates before meeting him. Everyone was sharing their thoughts about the hostel and the bizarre rumours they had heard. Then, I came back to my room, and I was not very proud of what I did next. Somehow, I knew that behind that door was a guy terrified of ragging, and a senior entering the room would answer all my questions. So, I (the fake senior) entered the room confidently and asked for his name and introduction. The boy stood at attention and said, 'My name is Yash Shetty. I am from Kalyan, Mumbai.'

'Since when has Kalyan become Mumbai?' I exclaimed loudly. Yash got scared. At this point, I couldn't hold back watching his terrified face, so I started laughing and said, 'Hey, I'm your roommate, chill out. I'm just having some fun!' Yash dropped in tears, and I got worried and asked for forgiveness. However, he reassured me that his tears were not because of me. Actually, he had been facing some issues at home for a long time. He wasn't worried about this place or the anticipated ragging. In fact, he mentioned that he was happier to stay in the hostel instead of spending endless nights trying to resolve his parents' arguments. But even though he was relieved to get away, he was worrying about his mother who recently told him how lonely she'd been feeling and she needed some friends. Yash was uncertain if he would be able to make friends himself, let alone for his mother. Unexpectedly he started searching on Google how to find his mummy friends– unfortunately, he got MILF reviews instead.

After a while, Yash and I left to meet our batchmates, Vivaan and Zeeshan, who had arrived in the room next door to us. Zeeshan was nicknamed 'Captain Cuddles'. He chose this name for himself because it reminded him of his weight loss journey. Once a very overweight guy who used to get bullied at school, Zeeshan had decided to lose his weight, and his transformation was inspiring. Zeeshan is well-built now with an impressive upper body. When I first met him, I could appreciate the strong grip in his hands after a handshake, but surprisingly, Zeeshan was more scared, expressing his concern about being bullied. I realised the stereotype of bodybuilders always being strong and stoic could sometimes overlook their vulnerability. On the other hand, Vivaan was slim with a visible bone structure. He remained calm and collected, consoling Zeeshan that they would most likely just be asked to take off their clothes during bullying sessions. He even removed his t-shirt, shouting while twirling it in the air, 'We'll see what happens!'

In the evening, all first-year students were called to the common room by one of our batchmates, Subhramanyam. He advised us to wear only formal and keep our heads down. I saw seniors standing in the common room propped us casually against the railings. I don't know about doctors, but they definitely came off to me looking like contractors asking for their weekly cut. I didn't want to be their fodder on the very first day, so I kept my head down right from the beginning. 'There are 4 seniors; I can count 8 legs,' I counted.

The seniors introduced us to the hostel rules for the 1st year students.

1. You have to wear formal, including a full shirt and pants all the time, even when a senior calls you at 2 am. Yes, wear formal shoes even when you go to the loo.

5. 5

2. You have to look at your shirt's third button while talking to a senior.

3. You always wish your seniors. If there are four seniors, you wish each of them separately.

4. You have to know the name of every senior, their hometown, their girlfriend's name, their preferred girlfriend's name, and their crush's name.

There were around fifty juniors and four seniors, still, we were the ones who were feeling insecure. We were all called one by one to introduce ourselves, and those who hesitated or broke the above rules had to start again.

After giving our introductions, we were ordered to collect the names of our girl batchmates who belonged to our hometown and submit them to our seniors— just as inmates, in jails, are given clear instructions about what to do and what not, we were instructed the same way. We knew that revealing anything private about ourselves could land us into a big trouble, so we had a 'No Sir', and 'Yes Sir' reply for every question.

5. 5

How many of you have girlfriends?

 Nobody raises their hands.

Does anyone consume alcohol?

Only Vivaan raises his hand. He was the junior with unnecessary tantrums, asking for special attention as exclaimed by our seniors.

Seniors: 'There will be a party, and only you will be allowed to drink.' Hearing this, everybody raised their hands!

After the general introduction, we were introduced to the hostel oath. The position to take the oath was to squat (when your knees do not exceed the level of your greater toe) and have your hands on your crotch. I can't pen down the oath here because it has words that are quite inappropriate for this book, but if you're truly curious, as you should be, then write to us at the e-mail address provided at the beginning of the book.

5. 5

By the next morning, stories of ragging had spread among boys and girls through a common group. The curfew for girls in the girls' hostel was 10 pm. But for the first-year students, the seniors kept it at 8 pm. All girls must wear a dupatta whenever they go out, no matter what they were wearing! The seniors found one rebel girl during the ragging session. Her name was Medhavi. She didn't want to wear a dupatta. She asked the seniors for another option. Sensing how hesitant she was at first to speak for herself the seniors came with a task for her thinking she wouldn't have the confidence to do it. The reward for completing the task was being exempted from ragging for the rest of the year. Medhavi was handed a condom; if she gave it to a guy, then she wouldn't have to wear a dupatta for the entire year. She went outside the campus wearing a lab coat and sold it to a guy saying, 'Save yourself from STDs,' and the guy took the condom. She was excused from ragging for the entire year but later realised that there was technically no ragging in the girls' hostel— just some rules that she still had to follow. On the first day of our college, we saw our warden for the first time, and probably the last time. And that was it. He rarely came to

5. 5

the hostel. Our seniors had even made a poster saying '*LAAPATA HAI*' with his images. It was hung on the common room wall. The warden passed by the poster every year but never cared to take it off or complain about it. Everything was managed by our Rector Gagan Sir. Gagan Sir was tall with a muscular build and a moustache. He was responsible for maintaining balance in ragging sessions, as any complaints to the administration could lead to his expulsion.

Our lectures started the next day. The college arranged a bus for the first-year students to help them avoid ragging. The first class was an introductory class on Community Medicine by Prof. Dr. S. N. Rao. He didn't pass professor vibes at all, instead, it felt like our own grandfather was here to teach us. He was too old to give a fuck about who was giving proxies, but too young to address who was late for the class. Girls and boys were not allowed to sit together in the first year. The girls used to come for lectures on time to occupy the window-side seats. All the boys were initially disappointed by this decision but were

5. 5

eventually happy as they didn't have to face temperature fluctuations throughout the year. The lecture hall experience was something new for me because I had no idea that most teachers took classes as if they were presenting a seminar. The rule was simple: start reading from the first slide and only look up at the end. Only a few cared if you were following along or not. We were excited to speak to the girls of our batch but before we could make any move, all the girls we admired were in a relationship with our seniors. Few of our batchmates were determined to start a relationship despite all odds.

Harshil and Chhavi were the first couple of our batch. It was shocking to see Chhavi falling for Harshil because after seeing his bizarre food combinations, it was difficult to even be friends with him, let alone kiss the lips which had touched such weird combinations. His weird combos included a papaya milkshake with orange cream biscuit, French fries with ice-cream, pizza and pineapple, and hot sauce on fruit. When it came to matching food, he right-swiped everyone.

5. 5

The only way to avoid ragging was to follow the bus route for the commute. But a few of my batchmates tried to be oversmart and ended up getting ragged. The next day, Zeeshan and I decided to skip the bus route and walk to our hostel. The main road outside the college campus was lined with tea stalls and motels on both sides. Every shop felt like a new hurdle to pass, as these were also the favourite hangout spots of our seniors. We decided that we would look straight ahead and cross the road as fast as we could, but 'Curiosity kills the Cat'.

One of our batchmates, PJ (Praveen Jumnani) was giving ragging to a senior (he was asked to sit like a hen and give eggs) as he didn't know the name of the senior. Zeeshan saw this and secretly whispered the name of the senior, 'Abhishek Valvi' to PJ. PJ said the name, but it turned out to be wrong, so he got ragged further. The senior asked who told him the name but PJ didn't reveal Zeeshan's name. Zeeshan then remembered that the name was Lay Joshi and uttered it. Again the name was not correct. PJ got ragged further, and now he had to even walk like a hen. We somehow escaped the situation and came back to our hostel where we experienced two different coping mechanisms — mine was telling this story to fellow batchmates, and Zeeshan went to sleep.

Zeeshan was blessed with deep sleep. Once he was asleep, nothing could wake him up. When PJ returned from ragging, he slapped Zeeshan twice, but due to Zeeshan's deep sleep, he remained unaware of this act of violence. Every night, we played cards on Zeeshan's back due to the lack of tables, making the game more interesting and when we got tired of holding cards, we could stick them in his Caboose Canyon.

In the hostel, we could be randomly called anytime at night for parties, usually when some seniors were celebrating their birthdays or they just wanted us to entertain them. These parties were extremely bizarre. I always saw one senior guy playing tennis alone with rackets to check whether he was high! After dancing for a while, the seniors got tired, and then they practised sitting and just moving their legs to dance, and we, the juniors, were asked to dance properly based on their footsteps. It looked like a dance class. At one of the parties, we saw Appa for the first time.

Appa was the senior-most resident of our hostel. He had a strong, commanding presence in a crowd. He always preferred high-collared coats or jackets, with gold chains or rings and a cigar in hand. You could clearly appreciate his cracked lips and blemishes on the skin due to excessive smoking. He had not passed his final exams because he demanded an apology from the dean of our college for allegedly suspending him for his misbehaviour with professors. Appa, who was once famous for ragging juniors, decided last year to voluntarily retire from indulging in such activities. He was now a member of the Anti-Ragging Cell of the college and frequently gave spiritual lessons to his juniors.

The following day, we were all invited to Appa's birthday. The host made a toast, welcomed everyone and shared a funny story that this was his 10th year celebrating his birthday in this hostel. We played games such as Fashion Police, karaoke, hidden talent and celebrity impersonations. I excelled in all these games and was invited to Appa's room. There I saw Appa sitting on his throne which was basically a reclining chair that you can see in OPDs. He had the surprise gift kept on the table. Appa handed the present to me saying 'This will be your companion in hard times'. I opened it immediately, expecting a treasure but I was startled as the gift was a McDonald's voucher. Appa lit up with pride thinking he had handed over a badge of honour to his junior. He started insisting that I join him for drinks. He then started to dance like crazy. Nobody could dance in a two-metre radius around him as his moves could critically injure people near him. He asked me if I had made friends and allowed me to bring them in for drinks. I rushed downstairs to call Yash, Zeeshan and Vivaan. Yash was busy in one corner of the common room with his phone. I asked him what was wrong, and he told me that he got a text message from his mom, 'Tell your dad that I will be late from work today. He will be happy to get this message.' Yash couldn't control himself anymore, and said, *'Mother's eye, my timetable, we will roam around all night.'* Our plan of having a night out was thwarted by

5. 5

Gagan Sir as he wanted us to make our parents call him asking for permission. Since we were new to hostel life and we didn't wish to grab attention for a small request, so we decided to enjoy Appa's offer for drinks.

The night unfolded into a chaotic scene of ragging rituals, with activities ranging from memorising room numbers and reciting batch oaths to simultaneous dance practices. The night progressed with Appa, fully intoxicated, demanding the names, room numbers, and batches of every senior present. Our blood alcohol concentration was likely above 0.16% that night.

Eventually, after getting bored, Appa called Gagan Sir, insisting that ragging was underway. Gagan Sir, capturing the entire episode on record, indulged in Appa's request for solo dancing, accompanied by a bottle of Bombay Sapphire Gin. Unsatisfied, Appa destroyed his attempt to take a selfie, asserting his dominance and threatening repercussions for anyone daring to complain.

5. 5

As the night fell, juniors were tasked with shouting abuses at a tree until a leaf fell, which granted permission to return to their rooms. We thought that this was impossible to achieve but we were lucky. The wind intervened, and it touched the tree as if it had invisible fingers causing sound-like murmurs, further causing a leaf to descend and signalling the end of the ragging session. Appa fully intoxicated said, 'Crazy to think there's this invisible force pulling everything down, like a cosmic magnet or something.' Finally, we were allowed to go back to our rooms where we could get some rest. Our feet were numb, our knees were sore and our hopes were withering.

I, Zeeshan, and Vivaan were determined to establish a distinct knock pattern to identify who was entering our room and prevent seniors from barging in for ragging sessions. Our efforts, however, were in vain as the seniors bypassed knocking altogether, opting to break down our doors to initiate ragging for the pre-freshers. After some time, the knocks at our door and our getting out of beds

5. 5

became synchronised. With time, the third-button rule shifted. We would still look at the third button, but instead, of ours, we would now look at our seniors. The loud greetings of the day soon shifted to simple nods on passing by a senior.

Our class WhatsApp group 'White Coat Legends' buzzed with excitement as we received the first message about our upcoming White Coat ceremony. The notice outlined the dress code for the first-year students – sky blue shirt, navy blue pants, and black leather shoes whereas for girls it was suit with compulsory dupatta. The ceremony was scheduled for Saturday, including receiving our white coats from the Honourable Dean Dr. Prof. (Emeritus) N. Kamte, along with other esteemed guests.

Upon arriving at the auditorium complex, a middle-aged man with round spectacles and frizzy hair greeted us, asking about the food quality at our hostel and expressing confidence in our future contributions to society. We assumed that he was an administrative staff member. PJ, addicted to taking selfies, took a selfie with the entire batch. The auditorium was decorated like a kingdom. The seniors wore suits and the juniors were in formals. First, we had to take the oath. Initially, everybody bent with their hands on the crotch, thinking it was the hostel oath, but then we realised our mistake and stood straight. We followed the teacher and chanted the Hippocratic Oath.

During the ceremony, we were introduced to various heads of departments. To our surprise, the man who greeted us outside the auditorium turned out to be the head of the psychiatry department.

As the speech began, I strategically chose a backseat to avoid attention and pretended to be engrossed in my phone. After a forty-minute speech by the dean, the Head of the Psychiatry Department, who was introduced by our dean as Dr. Dhawan, was invited to the stage to discuss work-life balance among medical students.

5. 5

In a memorable ten-minute speech, he shared personal anecdotes. He told us that his name is Dr. (Prof.) Maj. Kartikeya Dhawan. He emphasised the importance of being a kind person and the challenges of navigating the balance between mind and conscience.

He asked, 'Which one is important—learning the course of the ulnar nerve or preparing a perfect smear? He said that I would say everything is important. But one step at a time. He said, 'Our first task will be to differentiate between normal and abnormal. In the initial years, you will develop judgement power, but when you dive more into this science, you will realise that normal is subjective. A cancer patient getting her hair back feels she is returning to normal, whereas, for a normal healthy person, this might be nothing to celebrate.'

He encouraged us to find peace and satisfaction in our work, advising us to engage in tasks that bring joy without constantly watching the clock. The Head of Psychiatry concluded with a warm farewell, assuring us of his support anytime. The audience responded with a big round of applause, and a lunch break followed. Some students dismissed the importance of mental health, while others made light of it.

Unusually quiet, I attributed it to hunger when my roommate inquired about my well-being. We all devoured lunch like hungry monsters.

The monotonous life of class and practicals made me and my friends ponder the thought of entering into a relationship. As our batch was divided into two groups, A and B, our practical schedule was different. So basically we only knew half the population, and in that half, only a quarter of the population were girls, and in that quarter, only an eighth were shortlisted as potential future girlfriends. Feeling like there was too much competition, I was the first one to back out. Instead, I thought of making some nerd friends who'd help me out with my studies, and I found out that there was a girl named Natasha in Section A, who was the top scorer in the UG admission this year.

5. 5

So, I decided to send her a friend request, which unfortunately wasn't accepted. I didn't mention about this to my friends, but it did play on my ego a little and I took a vow to never speak to her. On the other hand, Zeeshan seemed optimistic. Even after linking up rumours of his crush, Jlo with seniors, he asked her out after college. Jlo was beautiful with a curvy figure, long brown hair and deep-brown eyes. She would never care whether you were paying attention to what she was saying; she would still say it.

As stepping out of the campus was not allowed for first-year students, Zeeshan planned his first date in the college canteen and accompanied me, as he knew he needed someone to initiate conversation. Zeeshan, online and offline, was two different people. Online, Zeeshan was surely Batman, but offline, he was a guy learning to hold his bat.

Jlo brought all her friends on her first date, I said to Zeeshan, 'You are being fooled.' Zeeshan ignored me, focusing on Jlo. Understanding my defeat, I told the canteen guy, 'You can see what's happening is wrong, right?' The canteen guy said, 'Yes.'

I said, 'Then why don't you say anything?' He said, 'Our business runs because of such fools.'

After brief introductions and ordering unnecessarily too much food for them, which I was never going to eat or pay for, I left the canteen and gave Zeeshan some space.

The next day at the college, when we were seated next to each other, I got to know his first date experience. To avoid getting caught by faculty, we were chatting on the back page of my notebook. Struggling with trying to convince Zeeshan to think before continuing with this relationship, I decided to let it go and focus on the lecture. However, this one statement that Zeeshan made that day stuck with me for a while. He said, 'Nobody who truly loves does reasonable shit, Jai.'

The second half of the classes used to be very exhausting for us as going again to attend the classes after lunch wasn't easy. We only got forty-five minutes, and the

5. 5

remaining fifteen minutes were spent commuting. We started physiology practicals in the haematology lab in which the first hour was hectic because we had to prepare smears. In the next hour, we could take a short nap or do some extracurricular as professors used to leave and lab assistants took over the lab. I mostly devoted that time to writing. The first thing I wrote in my diary was about the professors at my college. Each professor in our college had a distinct personality.

Lectures By—

Payal Ma'am: She teaches us Biochemistry and has a 300-page PDF in her pen drive through which she is going to teach the whole year. She gives the same lecture and teaches the same portion for decades. My seniors would easily guess what topic she must be teaching that week. She always appreciates the students of previous batches and hopes for even better students next year.

5. 5

Sagar Sir: He teaches us Anatomy and believes that English is a very funny language. His lectures would sound like this, 'These lessons are very important guys. You have to work hard. Tears will come out of your eyes like a waterfall, but you don't stop. You don't stop till you learn guys! We start with brachial plexus guys.' He would motivate us so sweetly that it brought no adrenaline rush whatsoever.

Meghna Ma'am: She is the sweetest teacher in Physiology. She makes a frog's leg with a handkerchief as teaching muscle physiology to animals isn't allowed anymore.

Basu Sir: He is a retired professor who is really passionate about the subject, Anatomy. The most encouraging teacher in the department. He is always motivating and says, 'You will be able to do it, just keep practising.' Anatomy is a subject in which you need to write it five times in order to memorise it. Read Cunningham's Anatomy.

5. 5

A sunny day in January was an aberration. But we had no holidays. We took our spiritless souls back to the class. The professor's lecture was full of abstruse theories. We were asked to bring a dissection kit but only one girl brought all the listed items. She bought all the accoutrements needed for practicals. I was frustrated that because of her we were going to be scolded. I tried to persuade her to hide the equipment but our debate turned acrimonious quickly. She had a bull-headed belief that she was right (hate to admit that she was) .

Dr. Basu, our anatomy professor called one of us to assist him in the dissection process before everyone was called to study.

Natasha accepted the invitation to perform the dissection with willingness. We realised that the story seniors told us about the dissection hall that it was haunted wasn't true. We didn't hear any absurd noises as they had mentioned. I observed how Natasha was fastidious during the dissection process. Our batchmate, Subhramanyam's foible was to interrupt and ask the same questions again and again to impress professors. The students used to sit in groups of 5-6 at separate locations in the dissection halls. Honestly, some groups were garrulous. Some hapless students who were forced to stand behind because of their height couldn't get a glimpse of what was happening. They relied heavily on video recordings of which Jlo was an expert.

After spending an hour in the dissection hall, we felt too lethargic to do anything. All we could do was wait for the practicals to end.

Our batchmate, Medhavita had kaleidoscopic thoughts. For some time, she had a headache and wanted to rest and after some time, she was angry that she was left behind in the dissection class. After some time, the teachers started ignoring what Subhramanyam was saying; their laconic reply hinted at their displeasure at Subhramanyam's interruptions.

5. 5

But Subhramanyam remained adamant despite all of this. Even Dr. Basu's pedantic comments on our anatomical knowledge were tiresome. Sitting in the dissection hall, I used to think how Dr. Dhawan's quixotic dreams of saving medicos from mental distress were inspiring. The sagacious old man used to share his advice freely with everyone.

Both my friends, Vivaan and Zeeshan contributed significantly to the hostel. Zeeshan primarily helped in the canteen by breaking bricks-like tortillas (*chapati*) for everyone. Also, he had a great vision. So he could catch paneer in the gigantic vessels of gravy and serve some lucky ones who were in the mess at the same time. People started tracking when Zeeshan went to the mess so that they could enjoy some paneer and broken chapatis, while Vivaan assisted in the 'go green' room. Despite his habit of smoking throughout the day, Vivaan lit a matchstick far away from himself, considering the initial flames to be cancerous. He asked people to turn off Good Night as it is also deemed cancerous.

5. 5

Having a friend who is in a relationship in the same batch has some advantages. We would get gossip about friend groups, fights, new couples, etc. We got to know that the girls had formed a mess group to keep each other updated on the food that is served every day. They did this to plan their meals accordingly as they didn't want to miss out on any delicious dishes. The group helped them stay informed about the menu and prevent any food wastage. Generally, the way boys celebrate birthdays is quite different from girls. Here, we followed a unique tradition where we broke eggs on the birthday boy's head, smeared cake on his face, and made him drink whiskey straight until he couldn't take it anymore. It looked more like a torture than a celebration, but this was how they liked to celebrate birthdays. After the birthday boy cut the cake, everyone rushed to get their share, and the cake disappeared in seconds. On the other hand, girls take birthdays seriously and make sure everything is perfect. They decorate the place with the best decorations, order the best cake, and prepare the best food. They believe in celebrating birthdays in a way that leaves everyone happy and satisfied.

5. 5

We had our first semester exams after three months of joining the college. Everybody who was reading standard textbooks finally shifted to basic textbooks. Some procured notes from seniors, some made their own and some like me considered the whole book as a note (Appa was really happy with my development in the hostel after knowing this.). Zeeshan used to study with Jlo over the phone where he had to explain the same topic to all her friends as well. He once accompanied me to the girls' hostel the day before our exams to deliver a photocopy of his notes to Jlo.

Meeting Jlo before exams helped because knowing about her preparation worked like a cardioversion for me. Jlo convinced me that if professors decided to fail someone, it had to be her. After all, she needed to know a day before the exam if the chapter 'Haemostasis' was covered in BD Chaurasia.

Before the theory exams, we got a lot of guidance from the seniors. The common advice was not to leave our paper empty and unfilled and to write anything related even when we didn't know about the topic. After each paper, we would guess the least number we could get in the question and if that exceeded passing marks, our paper was satisfactory.

In the first year, our primary focus was on Anatomy. If there was a two-day gap for Physiology practicals, everyone would revise Anatomy on the first day. Learning Anatomy was a group task. There were few people who by god's grace memorised faster than others and could teach fellow batchmates as well, and hence I learned adductor canal in Room 105, clavipectoral fascia in Room 120 and histology diagram identification in Room 117.

I remember when I was a child my elder cousins would challenge me in a Finger Vanish game where we had to identify the middle finger of the wrist. Very rarely I succeeded. The same thing was with arteries and nerves on the cadaver. You could see them, feel them and learn

5. 5

about them a hundred times, but when you are asked to show them in the viva, you get confused.

Anatomy practicals gave us memories for a lifetime because some of the answers we gave were epic.

The examiner asked, 'What are the layers of the spermatic cord?'

Yash replied, 'Exoderm, mesoderm, and endoderm.'

FAIL!

(DISCLAIMER: IF YOU ARE A MEDICAL STUDENT THEN YOU KNOW HOW BAD AN ANSWER IT WAS!)

We got to see two different personalities of some teachers during exams— the sweet and caring one during lectures but had come prepared with all the nasty questions and the strict professional motivated us when we were not answering.

5. 5

I passed two out of three subjects, failing my Biochemistry practicals by two marks— all because of having friends like Jlo. Only a few people would get samples with abnormal constituents of urine for exams, but those few lucky ones were me and Jaspreet. We failed our practicals for allegedly mixing a purple colour with the Rothera's test (a test to detect ketone bodies in urine; a purple ring formed indicates the presence of ketone bodies). The whole sample turned purple and therefore we claimed the patient must be suffering from some porphyria. However, that made things worse since it was a synthetic solution.

CHAPTER 2

THE FIRST SYMPTOMS OF LOVE

I was too slumped to attend Physiology practicals so I decided to take the second half off on the upcoming Saturday. Zeeshan and Yash had decided to skip the practicals and wanted me to join them. But I was reminded of what Arjun Bhaiya had advised me: only skip classes when you're going home, otherwise it will affect your attendance. The first half of the practicals was daunting as we were asked to prick our fingers for blood samples and make a tongue-shaped smear on a slide. First, I was hesitant to prick and torture myself, so I asked Subhramanyam. He was conveniently distributing his blood among our female colleagues but he denied helping me out, and said, 'This isn't a blood bank store. Go and take out your own.' I was shocked by this response as this was the same guy who came up to my room last night asking for biochemistry notes, talking to me sweetly like I was his crush. Nevertheless, feeling a little heartbroken and used in this relationship with Subhramanyam, I decided to prick out my own blood. To be honest, it was not that difficult, and I felt disappointed that I asked Subhramanyam. There were about fifteen minutes left in practicals to end when I saw some seniors gathering outside our practical hall. I thought we were screwed. Maybe I should have listened to my friends and skipped practicals, but out of all the seniors out there, one ma'am entered the hall followed by two more seniors. She held the position of the General Secretary at our college Cultural Committee, the first woman to hold such a position. She briefed us about the upcoming fresher's ceremony. Adhering to the protocol of avoiding direct eye contact with seniors to deter ragging, I found it impossible not to steal a glance from my corner window seat in the lab. The girl in front of me was adorned in a light pink suit with a dupatta, complete with glasses, brown curly hair, and, to my joy, dimples. Little did I know, my unabashed staring hadn't gone unnoticed. She playfully quipped, '*Janab*, do you need an invitation to look down?' My embarrassment prompted a swift shift in my attention. She then announced that there were two vacant positions on the cultural committee and they were planning to direct a short film with a small budget on medical life. Those interested could raise their hands. Anticipating fears of potential ragging during the selection procedure, nobody raised their hands. But without a second thought, I raised mine. I thought being the son of a film director would be of some advantage. To my surprise, Medhavi, the reserved girl who preferred solitude even in the hostel, also raised hers. Afreen expressed relief that only two had volunteered and said, '*Khuda ka shukr hai do hi bando ne hath khada kiya, khamakha hum pareshan hote.*' She took Medhavi's and my name, anticipating my involvement with a playful remark. The first senior to treat you with warmth in your college life earns your respect, and for me that was Afreen. After being selected for the cultural committee, we were invited to attend the orientation meet at the college auditorium. After the classes were over, I rushed towards the auditorium and saw that Medhavi was already making her way there. I started walking fast to catch up with her and as she turned around I waved at her, 'Hello, I'm Jai. Are you heading to the auditorium?', she nodded. Trying to make conversation, I asked her about her college life, where she was from, and if she was preparing for our upcoming Anatomy Class test. All her answers were in a single syllable – Yes or No. She didn't seem interested in telling me about her and seemed even less interested in getting to know me. As we reached the auditorium, she opened the door for herself but I crossed her and entered first. She gave me an annoyed look and I said, 'Thank you, Medhavi.'

As soon as we entered, the seniors spotted us and one of them shouted from a distance, 'You two, first year, come inside', other seniors shouted, '3rd Button' and 'It's been only 15 days and they're entering like a couple'. The other one said, 'Come here and introduce yourself.' Medhavi and I took the centre stage. One senior said, 'Ladies first.' Medhavi was scared. I could see her legs were shaking. She started her introduction.

'Hello, my name is Medhavi, I'm from Amritsar. I've done my 12th from St. Mary's Academy and my hobby is poetry writing.'

5. 5

Our seniors didn't seem too convinced. They asked her to be 'vocal for local' and say the same thing in Punjabi. After that, she was asked to make a rap song on Basu Sir (Anatomy professor), and if she failed to do so, she wouldn't be allowed to take part in any cultural events of the college. Medhavi started sweating and seeing this, and now even I was frightened. We both had lost all hope of being saved here and on the other hand, I couldn't let this position go as this was my only accessible chance in college life to direct a short film.

Medhavi had already started preparing a rap on Basu Sir. I could see her murmuring beside me. All I could sense from what I could hear from her mouth was that I didn't need to watch my favourite 'Tarak Mehta Ka Oolta Chasma' today because she was going to bring full-on entertainment with her rap today.

Before a chain of hilarious reactions could start, we had a visitor in the auditorium, and I heard the voice from the back door. 'What on the earth are you guys doing here? Is all the work over?'

Kaam ki izzat karna nahi jante aap log, chaliye aap dono niche jake baithe (referring to Medhavi and me).

I immediately recognised this voice, sweet but with a twist of command. This was Afreen.

As soon as we reached downstairs to grab a chair, she came following us and apologised for whatever happened in her absence. She also warned other members of the committee that if the ragging scene came up again, she would take strict action against them.

She turned towards me and said, 'So *janab*, Verma right? Jai Verma?

'Yes, Ma'am.'

I like to be called 'Afreen'.

Medhavi, Yes Ma'am!

'Afreen. It's not a tough name for you guys, is it?'

'No, Afreen,' I said.

She said, 'See, Director Sir is already in action mode.' She giggled and continued, 'So your father is a film director, you must know about films, right?'

'Yes, of course, I do Afreen.'

'So, what do you think will be better, SLR (Single lens reflex) or TLR (Twin Lens Reflex) cameras?'

I had no answer because I was a fan of movies, of Bollywood, of Bacchan, of Shahrukh, but never had shown any interest in filmmaking details. For me, filmmaking was all about the chemistry between a director and an actor. I never accompanied Dad at his shoots. He believed that filmmaking wouldn't be a match for me. What he wished for me was to have a stable career and family life which he thought filmmakers fail to have.

But I needed to answer. After all, I was the son of a renowned Marathi filmmaker, Anand Verma. I said, 'Ahem TLR will be fine'...I can manage in any circumstance.

Afreen said, 'Well, then we need a good script, cast and crew, editors, set designers, everyone.... *Allah, kitna kaam karna hai*. And yes, all this work has to be done in a week's time.'

'Do you two need coffee?'

She didn't wait for our answers and ordered coffee for us. Medhavi felt relieved now. I bended close to her ears and said, *'Haar kar jitne wale ko baazigar kehte hai.'* I couldn't hear her rap but definitely learned some new Punjabi slang which she was using at me after my quirky statement.

I didn't know why she disliked me. Maybe now I didn't want to know. In college life, there are people you don't interact with much and what keeps us away is our prejudice, our generalised thinking because of our past. All that is missing with those people is communication, when you communicate, you realise there can be comparisons but the reality is always different.

But today Medhavi was in no mood to communicate. As Afreen and I got to know each other briefly, we started working on the short film together. However, I couldn't shake off the uneasy feeling in my gut about Medhavi joining us. Our past altercation in the auditorium still lingered in my mind, coupled with her tendency to contradict every idea I shared, making her presence highly unwelcome. Despite both of us lacking the necessary experience to direct a film, we still decided to take on the challenge. Although, to be honest, it wasn't difficult to become a volunteer in college; all you had to do was express your willingness. As we started working on the project, our initial focus was on finding the perfect locations to shoot the film, and we held auditions to cast the actors. Surprisingly, while instructing other actors on how to act, we discovered that we ourselves were better actors. Throughout the process, Afreen remained calm and composed, even when things didn't go as planned. Her presence was not only comforting but also inspiring, and I couldn't help but get mesmerised by her beauty. However, I realised that I needed to keep my developing feelings in check, considering she was my senior, and asking her out could get me into trouble.

We change a lot when we are pursuing someone we love. We become a different version of ourselves, especially when the person is out of our league like Afreen. She had an allergic reaction to dust and smoke, so I hadn't been smoking for the past week. I even avoided my friends who smoked in public, as I didn't want to be tempted. In fact, I was the one who insisted that our short film should have an anti-smoking message, as I truly believed that smoking kills.

In the early morning, I found solace in smoking, as it seemed to facilitate my bowel movements. Without a cigarette, the passage of stool felt obstructed, and so I developed a habit of smoking during those early hours. The dynamics of love perplex me still, as I contemplate whether it empowers an individual or merely instils confidence. However, one thing was certain: I underwent a transformation from the Jay I once was. I used to

5. 5

meticulously iron my shirts each day before heading to the auditorium. My attention to aesthetics grew, evident in the enhancement of my Instagram stories, which were now dedicated to showcasing my affection for animals—a passion inspired by Afreen, who adored them dearly. After our work hours, I would often spend time watching her feed bread to the neighbourhood dogs. One day, I decided to join in, attempting to emulate her serene demeanour. However, lacking her calming presence, I found myself being chased by a pack of dogs back to my hostel, a comical yet humbling experience. The disapproval from the seniors regarding my closeness to Afreen was palpable. Appa, always the orchestrator of social dynamics, would invite the interested seniors who relished the idea of ragging newcomers from all batches. He introduced me as 'the one who got wings'. The warnings echoed in my ears: they promised me hell for the next five years if I dared to pursue Afreen. But I didn't stop following her, enduring every trial thrown my way. Appa, in his peculiar way, used to say to me after ragging sessions that if I succeeded in winning Afreen's affections, he vowed to let me take his beloved bullet bike on our first date. Most of my interactions with Vivaan and Zeeshan

5. 5

occurred after dinner. Yet, despite my efforts, I couldn't devote the time our friendship demanded, and the strains began to show. Nowadays, college friendships often resemble transactions; each relationship carries its own implicit terms and conditions. Friendships can crumble unexpectedly, leaving us reeling from the sudden loss. We envision dancing at their weddings, sharing a lifetime of memories, only to find ourselves estranged. Communication falters, dinners become solitary affairs, and the once-shared intimacy fades into memory.

As the shoot was drawing to a close, I couldn't help feeling a sense of sadness that it would soon be over. Over the course of the shoot, I had become good friends with Afreen, my co-star. We had spent countless hours together rehearsing our lines, and our friendship had grown stronger with each passing day. However, I knew that our meetings would soon come to an end, and I felt conflicted about it. On one hand, I was excited to see the final product of our hard work, but on the other hand, I wasn't sure if Afreen felt the same way about me. I had started developing feelings for her, but I didn't want to ruin our friendship by confessing. Additionally, I had been so focused on the shoot that I neglected my other friends, and I felt terrible about it. To calm my nerves, I turned to a quote by A. A. Milne, Winnie-the-Pooh, and posted it on my WhatsApp story. The quote read, 'Rivers know this: there is no hurry. We shall get there someday.' When Afreen replied with, 'Yes, *Inshallah*, our short film will be out soon.' I couldn't help feeling a twinge of frustration. I wanted to tell her that it was not just 'our short film', but it was 'our story', ours......man! Despite my mixed emotions, I knew I had to be patient and see where fate would take me. I just hoped that Afreen would feel the same way about me as I did about her. The incident I'm about to recount here occurred days before the release of our short film. It was a late-night call with Afreen, as we meticulously planned the sequence of events for the upcoming day. Afreen and I had grown quite comfortable conversing with each other, and our discussion included our struggles with the NEET exams, our families, and our aspirations. Time slipped away unnoticed, and before I realised it, it was well past 2 in the night. Sensing the late hour, I suggested that Afreen should get some rest, but she expressed reluctance, citing her unease since her roommate was out of town. What followed next took me completely by surprise. It turned out that Afreen had a tendency to talk in her sleep, a fact I wasn't aware of until that moment. As she drifted into slumber over the phone call, she began uttering words that left me stunned. 'Jai, you're a good guy, and I really like you a lot.' 'Don't leave me here with these people,' she murmured. Her confession caught me off guard. While her words hinted at her affection for me, I couldn't be certain if she was conscious of what she was saying. Despite my suggestion that she get some rest, Afreen insisted that I stay on the call, emphasising her fondness for me and her reluctance to disconnect. Feeling unsure of what to do next, I impulsively flicked on the lights in my room, a gesture that seemed absurd given the circumstances. Nervousness clouded my judgment, but I pressed on, telling Afreen that there was something I needed to share with her. Encouraged by her urging, I summoned the courage to lay bare my feelings. Taking a deep breath, I said, 'Okay, Afreen, so.....so....'. Curiously, she prodded, 'So, so.....what?' With a trembling voice, I finally confessed, 'I love you.' The silence that followed was deafening. I anxiously waited for her response, unsure of what it would entail. Afreen eventually confirmed that she was still on the line, expressing surprise at her own sleep-induced utterances. Sensing that I could no longer conceal my emotions, I surrendered to the truth and admitted, 'Afreen, I love you.' It was a moment fraught with vulnerability, and I braced myself for whatever her reaction might be, knowing that I couldn't keep my feelings buried any longer. Afreen's voice trembled as she spoke, 'No, no, no Jay, I didn't mean that. Oh my God, we shouldn't have been on the phone for so long. I messed up things. I'm so sorry.' The guilt in her voice was palpable. My voice was suddenly calm and reassuring, 'Don't be sorry Afreen. I couldn't hold this feeling within me for so long. Our film shoot is over, and now we have no obligations to meet every day, but I can't imagine that happening.' I waited for her response. For a while, there was complete silence on the other end of the line. My mind was racing with thoughts, wondering if I had said too much, or if I had scared her off. I felt like I had lost everything, and the weight of that realisation was crushing me. I wanted to leave everything behind, go back home, and just cry about all this, but I knew I couldn't. I had to show strength, even when I totally lacked it. Finally, I gathered the courage to speak, 'So, I thi…" Before I could finish this sentence, Afreen interrupted. 'Let's do it.' I was taken aback, 'What?' 'Let's do this, this relationship thing,' Afreen said, her voice full of conviction. I was speechless. I put my phone on mute for a second, not wanting her to hear the tears in my voice. I felt like I suddenly had a purpose in life, and the happiness I felt was indescribable. It was as if I had just produced the first batch of crystal, like Walter White from Breaking Bad. Then on, Afreen and I would meet every day, and as we both were big food lovers, we started to think that we met just to grab some food. Hearing her voice over the phone in our conversations, I thought she could be a great singer, but after my repeated requests every day when she finally sang, I never promoted her singing talent. To be honest, I barely knew any Urdu, but I had learned some heavy and complex words to impress her. Coming along with Afreen initially depended a lot on luck, but sustaining the relationship wasn't easy. Firstly, she was my senior in college, and secondly, our religions were different. In the initial days of college, it wasn't easy hanging out with her; we were always under constant scrutiny. Every evening, I would drop her at the hostel, and leaving her halfway felt like I couldn't take my love to its destination. Honestly, I didn't want to miss any opportunity to be with her and to praise her. If you're in love and not talking about the moon and stars, then what kind of love is it? So, for all the folks getting into relationships, here are two things to keep in mind: first, think carefully before making promises at the beginning, and second, don't take every little thing too seriously, or it gets tough to sustain. Afreen and I both loved reading books; we would recommend books to each other, even if the other didn't always follow the recommendations. After the first semester break, there were a few holidays in college. I had planned to stay back, but Afreen wanted to go home as her younger sibling, Zoya had cleared her law entrance test and she had to accompany her as a local guardian for counselling sessions. What was unique about Afreen was that she never complained about her situation. She had so much to take care of, apart from her studies, and still maintained her calm demeanour. Zoya was quite different from her sister; she was playful and a bit of a mess, just like most younger siblings are. I thought, why not go to Delhi to drop Afreen? Initially, she hesitated because she was afraid her family might see us but finally ended up agreeing. I think I wanted to go to Delhi because I feel it's a city with a soul. The first place on our wishlist was Fakir Chand Bookstore in the Khan Market area. Being book lovers, it had to be at the top of our bucket list, as it's one of the oldest bookstores in the area.

It's important not to get carried away by everything food vloggers say; they often only show the best sides of food, much like how humans showcase only the good moments on social media. We visited some renowned restaurants in Old Delhi, but the experience wasn't extraordinary everywhere; there was nothing particularly special about their flavours. However, the Shahi Tukda was an exception. Growing up, we didn't need to stay at hotels in Delhi because we had relatives living there; in fact, almost everyone has some relatives residing in Delhi. Our short trip to Delhi finally came to an end and we were back to our unforgettable college life.

Sometimes, you just smile, not because the other person has caught you, but because they firmly believe you're a scoundrel, and even if you haven't made a mistake, all the blame falls on you. It always used to get uncomfortable when Afreen was too close. Usually, I could hide my emotions very well but few things found their way upwards. Afreen was clumsy, not a little, but to the extent that she would hurt herself sitting on the bed as if her limbs were some other species having their own senses and an anti-Afreen vibe. She always complained about why I laughed at first when she got hurt this way, but the history of the present illness of my beloved always amused me. Afreen grew up watching Hindi TV serials which had a great influence on her expectations. Her usual jibe whenever I disappointed her was *'Ya Allah isse jahannum naseeeb ho'.* (Oh God, may hell be his fate.) Do you love someone so much that you've given up hope they'll ever reciprocate or even come close? Have you ever felt that they might unintentionally hurt you because they don't love you the same way? It took me a long time to understand what kind of person Afreen was. Initially, I thought she was selfish and just wanted love without ever reciprocating it. But later I realised that you don't get love the same way you give. You have to work on your perception.

Afreen usually waited outside my lecture hall after her classes, which she wouldn't have been able to do otherwise, because she was after all my senior. However, she always said that ego should never come into personal relationships.

We also had intimate moments. But after Afreen said, 'There is nothing fulfilling about the experience Verma ji,' I remained in doubt. You realise that when you have sex for the first time, everything is naturally set to 0.5x speed. It's not as easy as video lectures to shift to 2x, as desired. Also, rather than being selfish about myself, I realised intimacy is about mutual efforts and understanding.

Isn't it amazing that in the initial years of a relationship in college, you just forget that other people exist? Every corner is a place for you to express love, whether it's the shady area of the canteen or the back seat of an auditorium. You get oblivious to your surroundings. But, as time passes by, you realise how stupid you've been, even though they were some of the most snap-worthy moments of your relationship, you are somehow forced to evolve.

Getting into a relationship is easy because in the initial stages, you just want that person in your life. You do many things to impress your partner and ignore many others. But when you start to assess the future, you take a lot of aspects into consideration. It could be family, goals, understanding and more. I used to like my own space despite being in a relationship because that allowed me to be more creative, but Afreen didn't agree with this idea after the first six months of our relationship. I thought we needed to give time to each other for personal goals because, after all, our careers were not on the same pitch. I think we all should accept the fact that relationships are not going to be the same forever. They will change with time. All relationships have an expiration day unless they evolve into marriage. But then again, marriages also seem to have an expiration date when divorces come into the picture— a hard pill to swallow, isn't it? But none of this takes away the love and affection you experience for each other. You just have other priorities, which, if ignored, will ultimately create more tension in your relationship.

5. 5

CHAPTER 3

THROUGH THE LENS

Finally, we got the opportunity to watch our short film on the big screen. All our hard work finally paid off.

Theme – 'THROUGH THE SCRUBS' (A voice came in the background.)

Come, let's listen to a story that will surely resonate with every medico's life, at least once.

DR. TUSHAR AS A MEDICINE RESIDENT

As a resident in MD Medicine, I chose to become a doctor because both my parents were in the medical field, and I wanted to follow in their footsteps...... (laughs). That's not the real reason. The actual reason stemmed from an incident that occurred a few years ago. It made me realise that I wanted to pursue this career for the rest of my life. There was an incident involving an 80-year-old woman with extremely frail hands, almost like wood. She was in intense pain and earnestly begged the doctor to perform surgery on her hands (The doctor I'm referring to is my father.). Her haemoglobin level was critically low, making the surgery risky, but the pain was unbearable. The only remaining option was to transfuse blood, proceed with the operation, and hope for the best. However, both her husband and another elderly person were thin and old themselves, and there was no one else available for blood donation. My father called me and asked me to bring different types of fruits. When I arrived there, I discovered that my father had personally donated blood to that lady. A complete stranger, yet he operated on her, expecting nothing in return. While sitting down for dinner that night, I asked my father, 'Why did you do that? It wasn't your responsibility or part of your job profile.' Dad replied, 'Son, when I entered this profession, I was told that it would demand my blood and sweat, and it was my privilege to live up to those words.' My respect for my father grew immensely. I immediately knew that I wanted to become a person like him, and that's why I became a doctor.

DR. NAINA AS AN OBGY RESIDENT

As an OBGY resident, it might sound cliché, but I always wanted to become a doctor, more specifically a gynaecologist. The idea first struck me at the age of 7 when my grandmother shared a story about how I, during my mother's delivery, inadvertently endangered my twin sister. She explained that my sister could have been saved if there had been a proper professional setup. Now, 25 years later, I find myself as an OBGY resident dealing with a rare monochorionic, monoamniotic twin case with complications. Preventing such occurrences is easier said than done, but I strive to do my best to ensure the health of both the mother and the baby. However, I'm aware that life and death are not entirely within our control. We are fighters, and we will continue to fight for the healthy outcomes of our patients. As an OBGY resident, you are trained to think logically. Pale nails, pale stools—numerous differential diagnoses arise. However, once the training concludes, you realise that the world, and life in general, are sheer chaos. The society operates on norms with vague boundaries. You're compelled to deliver the best services in resource-limited settings. With experience, you understand that your best may not always be enough, and gratitude is not always guaranteed. You normalise work trauma – being berated in emergencies, scolded for no fault, perhaps even being threatened or physically harmed becomes internalised. Because the next day, you must return to work, regardless. In this sea of people, you find yourself unable to share your pain, and it gradually erodes your mental peace. The darkest days are encapsulated in satirical pieces. Dark humour serves as both a comfort and a reminder to be cautious about the perils of not opening up. The sheer confidence in my written blog stems from the understanding that no one is reading it. Instead, they might take a leap of faith, seeking someone to share their trauma with, learning to save their own lives before others.

JAI AS AN ANESTHESIA RESIDENT

As an anaesthesia resident, you have to get used to being Mr. India because most people have no idea that we're medically qualified. I've been asked countless times about

5. 5

the qualifications needed to become an anaesthetist. Patients remember their surgeons' names but never ours. Nevertheless, it's an immensely rewarding job. We'll be found everywhere in the hospital—from the operating room and ICU to the ward, emergency department, and even pain clinics.

We assess patients' fitness for surgery, and the likelihood of complications, and support them through the operation and postoperative period. The first time I administered anaesthesia to a patient, it was terrifying. A small mistake could be fatal, considering our drugs suppress breathing, and it becomes our responsibility to take over that function. Even now, in certain situations, I feel fear, but I hide it, as staying calm is crucial to our job. During emergencies in the operating room, the entire team looks to the anaesthetist for leadership, as the surgeon is often too focused on fixing the immediate problem. Despite the challenges, specialising in anaesthesia is fulfilling, and a major adrenaline experience.

DR. ZAID AS A SURGERY RESIDENT

5. 5

The medical school was a blast, with friends who became family. Residency in the subcontinent, as everyone knows, sucks the last bit of ATP out of our system. Why? I have an answer. Every surgeon's nightmare is not finding what they went in for and what they read in their books. We call it varied anatomy. 'Life is indeed a Pandora's box, filled with unexpected challenges and surprises. All we can do is adapt and overcome them. So, don't be troubled by the problems you might be facing. Keep your friends close and beers cold. Cheers!'

INTERN

This incident occurred during my fourth-year MBBS practical exam in medicine, which was my favourite subject. I was given a case of stroke/brain haemorrhage. When it was my turn for the viva, I greeted the examiner, who then asked me which nerve facilitated my greeting. After some hesitation, I replied, 'Vagus nerve.' The examiner proceeded to ask me several more questions, most of which I managed to answer. However, after half an hour, he inquired about the boundaries of the pterygopalatine fossa, which I couldn't answer. I apologised, but he grew angry, questioning how I could not know this and expressing doubt about passing me. Abruptly, he took my exam paper and left. I was stunned. His harsh words were echoing in my mind. Back in the room with my batchmates, I silently packed my bag. A friend approached, asking how it went. I remained silent, and as his concern grew, I couldn't hold back any longer and burst into tears. (I must say……Those who claim that boys don't cry haven't met a medical student.) My batchmates tried to console me but it didn't help. I walked back to my hostel, called my mom and told her what had happened. She consoled me and said, '*Beta*, it's okay and keep trying until you succeed.' After a month, I saw the result and apparently, I was the topper. I laugh at this incident to date. Basically, my advice is, 'Don't take these exams so seriously that you get affected by them. Even though these exams hold importance, study hard for them, and learn as much as you can to help your future patients. But always remember that a result doesn't define you. I've seen medical students lose their morale over one failure, and a lot of times that one failure starts defining their entire professional journey. Ultimately, we're all going to be great doctors, just work hard.'

AFREEN AS A FINAL-YEAR STUDENT

Becoming a doctor in a family without any medical background has its unique advantages. While it may seem impressive on the surface, the absence of inspirational figures can pose challenges. Despite the love from family, there's a gap in understanding. Why did I choose medicine then? It appeared to be a promising career, a path where I could make a difference. Once when I was assisting a senior in a ward, a little girl approached me, expressing her dream of becoming a doctor just like me. That simple sentence held profound meaning. The realisation that I could inspire someone, especially a young girl to dream big. Encouraging her to pursue her dream became a significant moment for me. Reflecting on my journey, I never believed I could reach this point until I cracked NEET. I wished someone had told me I could, so I made sure to be that encouragement for her. That was the moment I fell in love with the profession. I knew that I was on the right path. Even coffee can't keep me up at night but interacting with patients does. The more I interacted with people, listened to their struggles and assured and treated them, the prouder I felt with this profession. I'm glad I fell in love with what I do because of my experiences and not just because it is considered a noble profession.

Listening to all these stories somewhere sparked motivation within us. It felt like a significant responsibility on our shoulders.

Now was the time for the quiz, where everyone seemed to know the questions, but even the ones creating the questions didn't know the answers. The winner of this quiz would receive the 'Bottle of the Year', which is essentially a Jack Daniel's bottle adorned with fairy lights.

The questions were as follows:

1. What disease is commonly seen on Valentine's Day?

2. What is Darling's disease caused by?

3. What is Gilchrist's disease caused by?

4. Where is Bull's eye maculopathy seen?

5. Where is Swimming pool conjunctivitis seen?

6. What are the causes of Blueberry muffin rash?

Honestly, nobody was quite interested in being a part of the quiz as everyone was still talking about our short film. Despite creating groups for the quiz, we were getting collective answers from everyone, and some of the answers turned out to be really funny. One person said that Darling's disease is caused by getting friend-zoned from your crush and another joked that Bull's eye maculopathy is obviously seen in bulls. Now it was time to announce the winner. Actually, the winner was the whole batch because everybody rushed to take one sip from the bottle. It is unique how cinema and challenges can unite us.

CHAPTER 4

TUG OF HEARTS & MINDS

While I was at home, my exam dates were announced for the next semester. I didn't know why, but every test I appeared in after entering college felt like a battle. It felt like I was studying and doing all this to prove something to someone.

Every time I returned to my hostel from home, my luggage got heavier from all the food Mom packed for me. Dad made sure he came to drop me at the station and didn't leave until the train departed. Mom would secretly give me extra pocket money every time I left for the hostel. To date, Dad isn't aware of this, and till today, I don't know how she managed to save up for me every time I came home.

Afreen's mother used to take tuitions after school hours. Although her family's financial condition was not that good,

5. 5

she still wouldn't take any charges for tuitions because she believed everyone should contribute in their own ways for the betterment of society with whatever resources they have. Afreen frequently quoted her lines—

'Education is important, even if you are not able to bring the change on your own. At least you must support those who work for it. Ideas work best when they are well exchanged, and nobody should be devoid of education due to family circumstances or poverty.'

I was given very little pocket money from home. I did a lot of *jugaad* to get money to go out with Afreen but the number of times I went out with Afreen, I also had to make time for my friends. I didn't want them to feel ignored as I was not able to give any time to them because of my relationship. Before I started dating, I remember how Subhramanyam came to our room and stated that this triangle of our friendship was going to break soon, after Jai fell in love.

In my second year, I was relieved that my seat in semesters was not in the first row. My seat was on the second-last bench, and on my right side was Saurbhi, aka Sorbbs. I couldn't believe my luck. Even if she turned a little towards her left, I would immediately stop writing and ask her if she needed any help, and if she did require help, I ensured to prioritise helping her with answers before writing my own. Sorbbs presence was captivating and unforgettable.

Afreen had two friends, Inaya and Aakriti. Aakriti was her roomie as well. They shared a great bond at the beginning of college life which ultimately turned sour with the years passing by. People who come from broken families know the importance of good and long-lasting relationships. Afreen never wished for the bond she had with her friends to get broken, but I think she blindly trusted them right from the beginning. I felt that this particular issue with her friends began to arise after I came into Afreeen's life. She would spend a lot of her time with me, as most partners do in a relationship, but was disapproved by her girlfriends. I could understand why they were bothered by this; however, it didn't justify some of their behaviour. Her friends became distant – they stopped inviting Afreen to parties. She wasn't trusted any more to share gossip with, and they even had a WhatsApp group called 'Cosmic Cuties', which Afreen wasn't a part of. And when Afreen learnt about this secret group, she was definitely annoyed and upset. What breaks trust in a relationship is when every member of the group knows exactly how they're behaving and still acts like everything is normal, like they assume this distance is normal. It's foolish to think that the person with whom you had spent a significant amount of time in your college, won't notice a change in your behaviour. They do, in fact, every word that comes out of your mouth, they now analyse it through their understanding of you. They don't like your jokes anymore.

I and Afreen had become physically distant after eight months of dating. I had to brush every time I wished to kiss her. We fought often over petty things like who was going to order food, what we were going to have, why the room was too messy, why I did not bathe every day and the list was too long. We slowly started losing the spark, and it all felt like a routine.

In the second year, we again spent sleepless nights but this time, we weren't that exhausted as we already knew how our days were going to be and I guess we all had become mentally stronger. Pharmacological classifications used to trouble us, especially cephalosporins. We realised that to pass the second year, we needed to study in groups. But I couldn't study in larger groups, so I decided to study with Subhramanyam. Apart from being the toxic male friend, he was also the alpha male in academics.

Yash again had the best answers in viva.

'What are the side effects of Ondansetron?'

Yash: Nausea and vomiting.

DISCLAIMER: Almost all drugs have side effects of nausea and vomiting, but Ondansetron is the drug of choice (Treatment) for vomiting!

We get confused every time between Salah and Klima needle.

The Head of the Department of Pathology was not an easy person to deal with. He would make us read what we had written in our exam papers, and believe me writing a wrong answer in theory, and reading it out loud in front of professors is not the same thing. The difference is like being naked in the washroom and being naked in the auditorium.

We used to have spotting viva for second-year subjects. In the spotting round, a buzzer was there which used to ring after every ten seconds, indicating that we had to move to the next spot. I was confused between MacConkey agar and Blood agar in the buzzer round, as they both look red, just different variants of red. So our batchmate, Sorbbs taught us the difference in the colour by different shades of a red lipstick in her purse.

In FMT Viva, 'What is the punishment for fake fitness certificate?'

Yash replies, 'Sir, fine and jail.'

Finally, we all passed our second-year final exams except for a few who couldn't clear Pharmacology.

We entered into our pre-final years and honestly, it was a much relaxing experience.

Ravi Sir, who taught us Ophthalmology, had many informers telling him who all smoked, who had broken up, and who partied last night and didn't study for postings. When he targeted a student, he sat alone, and four benches around him were always empty. When a student did not answer, he said, 'I know you had a breakup but that doesn't mean that you'll stop studying.' Even though he was a nosy professor, it turned out that he had a 100% passing rate for students in his department.

So the day was our '3rd ANNIVERSARY', but I had completely forgotten about it. It wasn't until afternoon that I realised this. But, as fate would have it, Afreen had already taken care of things. She had bought chocolates and a T-shirt as a surprise gift. It was a heartwarming gesture that touched our protagonist's heart. At the end of the day, it's the small things that matter the most. She shared this incident with her friends, Inaya and Aakriti, and of course, they weren't happy. They were smart enough to realise that such incidents happen but dumb enough to judge Afreen for being with me when I couldn't even do the bare minimum like remembering anniversaries. They even mocked Afreen. How could she take the first step to celebrate our anniversary? She should have made me feel guilty about it or maybe blocked me for a day or two. They said that if their partner had made this blunder, they would have immediately cut all ties. When I and Afreen met the next day, we discussed this. She told me that their partners had never done for them what I had done for Afreen when she was low. Inaya even had a moment where she was forced by her boyfriend, Sid to sleep with him. Aakriti always complained that her partner left when she felt low, but still, they continued their relationship. I never had a bad equation with her friends and never insulted them, but even then they had so much hate for our relationship. We realised that some people like to justify their troubled lives by creating more trouble everywhere possible. Her friends were not happy with their relationships so they didn't want us to be happy either.

CHAPTER 5
BROKEN VOWS

Life pulls you down every once in a while, so we do what we can to get by. Honestly, my life wasn't just throwing lemons at me, it decided to literally paint rocks as lemons and hurl them at me at 200 km/hour. Owing to my depressed mood, which had pretty much affected the environment in our tiny room, Vivaan came up with the idea to take the edge off. He managed to drag my broken ass, along with Zeeshan and Yash, for a drive to watch the sunset, as if the setting of the sun of my life wasn't enough. But for once I didn't want to cancel any plans as I had done the previous week. So with no specific plan and no money, I hauled myself into Vivaan's borrowed car. Zeeshan called shotgun and was the default 'passenger princess', fully exercising his self-declared right to the playlist and making us listen to Punjabi gym hits while Yash was practically begging to get off by the third song. Nonetheless, the drive was pretty pleasant after Yash had succumbed to his fate, frankly, we all had, and the destination was even prettier. I suppose we appreciate the little things even more when we take a moment to slow down. While I watched the scattered colours of the sunset, the orange mixed with the shades of blue and hints of pink, slowly merging into purples and reds, the peaks of the hill slopes tried to enclose the colours, reflecting and playing hide and seek with the clouds, just like my thoughts. Sitting on the hood of the car, I could see the light dimming, merging into darkness down below the cliff. The slow hum of a song none of us knew played on the car's speaker, and Vivaan handed me a joint. Zeeshan fetched a packet of cigarettes and Yash joined me on the hood, staring at the sun. The thin strings of smoke from our lights intertwined together like the silence of the untouched valleys beneath us. There was no breeze, there was no talking, and we watched the blend of colours, and for once in the span of the past week, I felt at peace. Yet, my life still felt trashed. I knew I had decisions to make soon. The decisions I didn't even want to think about, but like I had the choice, and even if I did, could I? I did not want to answer these questions, maybe for a few more moments. I wanted to live in this perfect moment. I might not have been grateful for a lot of things but at the moment, I was truly grateful for my friends, including Zeeshan's Punjabi gym hits playlist.

A packet of cigarettes and one joint later, we decided to head back. So far along the way, if you have come to know anything about Vivaan, you cannot threaten him with a good time judging by the trajectory of my life. I decided to completely flatten the edge and make an effort to ask myself to suck it. I decided to get high, on Lysergic Acid, LSD. Not my best move, but I had three other willing participants. I mean, bad decisions and we were pretty concurrent, but did we regret it? Maybe. Would we do it again? Hell, yes. On our way back, Yash apparently knew this peddler and got us a vial of LSD which against our better judgement, we decided to try while on the road. Zeeshan had the conscience to play some decent music. And while the drive back was along the same road, it didn't feel the same because I could swear I saw a dinosaur chasing us. I told Vivaan, 'Bhai! There's a dinosaur behind us.' Zeeshan said,

'No. That's the London Bridge with legs.' Vivaan and Yash peered outside their windows to confirm which one it was and stopped the car because they spotted a shop selling *pakoras*. And even though Zeeshan and I wanted to get out of there as soon as possible, we decided to focus on the *pakoras* first. After many detours and most things we did not remember, like what kind of *pakoras* we had, we made it back to the college. The next day, I decided to break things off with Afreen. While I didn't remember many things, I remembered one, the moment of clarity. Afreen and I had a lot of things in common and a lot of things uncommon and I loved her. I loved her a lot but this was the kind of love that had only one consummation. It was the kind of love that was meant to be doomed from the very beginning and somehow we were both aware of its imminent expiration. And this was going to break hearts, both mine and hers. While I wanted to fight for us, I would rather remember her as the light that made me love life than be filled with resentment towards her. I could not ask her to separate from her family and she wouldn't want that for me. I mean for whichever century we live in and for whichever

5. 5

generation we are a part of, societal pressure, family and our obligations still remain the priority.

We decided to meet at our usual hangout spot. It was funny as we had our first date there. This would be our last date if you could even call it a date. But unlike our first, I made no effort to dress up. I just wanted to get this over with. I had been arriving late most of the time to all our commitments but I was early today. While I waited for Afreen, I watched everyone around. A couple on their date was laughing and the guy couldn't take his eyes off her. There were two steaming cups of tea while my chilled glass of water had tiny droplets of condensed water on its surface. I turned my eyes away and took a sip of water while thinking of all the 'what ifs', staring at the still surface of water in my glass. Afreen sat in the chair opposite me, and I couldn't help but notice that she had makeup on. She wore white. She looked pretty, with her gentle wavy hair, curled lashes, glazed lips and the mole on her face. 'Hi', I said. She smiled and said, 'What are you thinking?'

'Nothing.'

'Did you order something?'

'The usual?'

5. 5

'Okay.'

Afreen went ahead to get our regular burgers, fries and coffee while I stared at her. We were being cordial after such a long time, and I almost changed my mind. I did not want to do this anymore. I thought I would see through it. I would somehow convince our families. We could make this work. We made small talk until our food arrived, and honestly, I was grateful for the music that had started playing in the background. My heart was beating a mile a minute. The calmer Afreen looked, the more anxious I felt. I felt a sense of impending doom. 'So, do we need to talk? You had been avoiding me for a week straight.'

'Afreen, I am sorry. I_.'

'You don't have to be. I understand. This has to happen.'

'What?'

'Don't do this. You had your mind set when you called to meet today.'

The waiter chose that exact moment to bring out our food, and I was grateful for the distraction. I had started to become grateful for many things these days. 'Do you guys need anything else?'", he asked.

'No, that'll be all.'

I wanted the waiter to sit with us for the entirety of the meal. Afreen didn't say anything further and instead chose to focus on eating— another common thing between us. And strangely, I did not have the appetite. The glazed skin of the burger with its sesame seeds felt like sand with each bite. The fries were extra salty but I stuffed my face like they were ears and chewed extra slow to delay myself from hearing the unpleasantries that Afreen was sure to speak. Afreen finished the last of her food while I was still stuck with half of my burger and signalled the waiter for the coffee. She watched me eat, and I couldn't look at her face. With a steaming cup of coffee in her hand and a smile, she cleared her throat and said, 'So....are you going to finish the food?'

'I am done.'

'It was good while it lasted,' she said with a sip.

'Don't do this.' I stared at my cup. I wanted to drown in it.

'You had been thinking about it too.'

'But I don't want to. I don't want to break up anymore.'

'We have to. I know you understand. It took a lot out of me to come here today. Please, let's not make this ugly, Jai.'

I wanted to cry. I was the one who had decided to break up. I called for this and yet now I wanted to erase the past one hour from my existence. What was I even thinking? The mismatched chairs at our table were hurting my eyes and the smile of the waiter made me want to punch his face. The evening sunlight streaming through the window was burning my arm. Afreen loved this table specifically for this, and on other days, I loved seeing the sunlight up her face. But today, I couldn't even look at her. She stood up and left, taking all the colours and light with her. 'Goodbye, Jai. Do good.' I stared back at her, hoping for a replay of those Bollywood movies where the heroine changes her mind halfway and runs back. But she didn't.

I stayed still in my seat and the waiter came over once again, 'Sir, do you need anything else?' I looked around and stood up, shaking my head. The couple in the opposite table had left. 'Goodbye, Afreen.' The sun had set. For the rest of the week, I tried my best to come to terms with what had happened. And like any grown man, when nothing else seemed to work, I decided to deal with my breakup playing GTA in the same clothes I had been wearing the night Afreen broke my heart. I was stinking, my side of the room was trashed with stale cigarette butts, cans of energy drinks and beers piled up among boxes of takeout and my unwashed clothes from weeks ago. GTA was supposed to help. I was going to play rashly, hit some random people, let off some steam, and let go of some of this pain inside my heart but instead, some old aunty who was clearly a better player than me had smashed me to my death. I lost and gave up and went off to sleep like I had an hour ago. While I'd been wallowing in my depths of self-pity and despair, contemplating my life decisions for the past few weeks, my old school friend, Navandeep decided to pay me a visit. He'd apparently fallen for a girl, who was a bit dominating which did not go well with Navandeep. And this is where I have to warn you that it was that time of the year, 'fielding season'. Love had officially warped itself from the air. Cupid was on vacation. Navandeep had a breakup but unlike me, he had the rizz. He had started dating another girl simultaneously, keeping things casual as if that ever worked out for anyone. But we gave him the benefit of the doubt. This girl embraced the persona of a perfect girlfriend for him and was absolutely head over heels for him. Classic Navandeep! And just like any classic complicated situation, Navandeep was friends with both his ex and current situationship. Why? Because he didn't believe in the concept of love. For him, love was a lie! I agreed but I doubt his self-proclaimed girlfriend would. This situationship now wanted a relationship; labels, tags and everything in between.

For once, I decided to try and take a break from my issues and asked Navandeep to hang out in my room. I genuinely felt that I could give him some moral support. Zeeshan and Vivaan were out running errands, and I realised that I hadn't seen them in the last few days. I had not done much the last couple of days, my unkempt hair, untidy clothes, the half-eaten box of pizza under my bed, and my entire corner of the room were evidence of that, and there was a distinct smell of something rotten. For a second, I felt maybe I should have cleaned up before Navandeep was here but he was already at the door staring at me in disgust. Navandeep said, 'When was the last time you had a shower?'

'Gonna take one right after you leave.'

'Bro, I just got here. You wanna chase me away?'

'I didn't say that.'

'Yeah, yeah, I misunderstood, sorry,' he snorted. 'I am going to cry. You were going to give me moral support.'

I sprayed an air freshener, lit a joint, and prepared to lend Navandeep moral support. 'So, what troubles you, my boy?'

All Navandeep had to say was, '*Behenchod*!' Tell me does it get any worse! I mean, what is this timing? Where was all this love when I actually had the heart for it? But as time has been a witness, things never happen as we like them. Navandeep's ex found out about his second girlfriend, and he was officially labelled as a cheater. Navandeep had a lot to say this time, '*Behenchod*! I am guilt-ridden if I accidentally kill a mosquito, and she calls me a cheater. She broke up with me and when I finally moved on with someone else, she decided to come back and mess with my head. If that wasn't enough, my new girl has found out about this and now she is calling me out as a molester! The one who was kissing me in every possible location in the city.'

'Be right back,' I said.

'Leave me, leave me alone.'

'I need to pee. I'll be back in 2 minutes, tops.'

'*Bhai hai tu mera*!' (You are my brother.)

And that is how you mend a friend's broken heart. I didn't get back in 2 minutes though. I had a full shower and by the time I got back, Navandeep was dead asleep on my dirty sheets that he had looked at with disgust. The thing with school friends is that they accept you the way you are.

That evening, I finally cleaned my room, inching my way towards normalcy. Did I mention it was the break-up season? Because in the span of two weeks, Vivaan was seen more in the room. His corner was getting messier while I had worked hard every day to fix mine. I was slowly on my way to give up on fixing the smell because while everything else was changing, this was one thing that remained constant. Those empty beer cans and takeout boxes had to be dealt with. But that was a long way to go without continuous nights of debauchery owing to nursing our broken hearts, whether that was fortunate or unfortunate is a question that will always be morally grey. We were downright addicted to getting high; hookah – alcohol – weed, you name it, and we had it. It was one of those nights. Beyond midnight, I had the urgent need to poop. It was urgent enough to make me disregard the location. Actually, I did regard the location, I just didn't care. I pulled down my pants and decided to go Amber Heard in my room. But what I didn't realise was that Appa Sir witnessed this from the second floor and this gem of a person, came all the way downstairs to pick up my pants and went as far as to put me to sleep. Needless to say, the next day when everyone woke up, there was an additional smell in the room. Fortunately for me, Zeeshan was the first one to wake up and his first response was, 'Yaar, a dog pooped in our room! To which I replied, 'Ew! We should've closed the door.

I said, bowing my head, 'I'll make sure to close the door every night now.'

Zeeshan went ahead to brush his teeth and thankfully told all the seniors his version of the story. I still thank God for this. I was mostly on drugs all day long and was mostly oblivious to what was happening around me. My plan to clean up my act had been put on hold for an indefinite amount of time. When did I make that decision? I couldn't remember. We were back to our nights of recklessness and days of messy corners but made it a point to shower at least every other day. And like I was forgetting most things, I forgot where I had kept my phone. After half an hour of upturning every possible location, I couldn't find it and by default, my best guess was either Vivaan or Zeeshan must've hidden it. I didn't want to give them the satisfaction of seeing me panic so I went on with my day casually, but finally when night fell, I couldn't help myself. I said, 'Whoever has my phone, time to bring it out.' Vivaan and Zeeshan simultaneously looked at each other and replied, 'Bro, we didn't do anything.'

'Fuck! Fuck!'

Vivaan and Zeeshan hugged me in sympathy because that was all they had to offer. But I still had my doubts about them and asked them twice again. We tried to go phone hunting but it was unsuccessful, so we got back to our rooms and spent the entire night getting high. I was at a very low point in my life and now I didn't even have my phone. Afreen was done with me. I hadn't attended any classes in quite a while. I lay on my bed looking at the ceiling, spotting cobwebs in the corner thinking. 'We need to clean that up.' I had been thinking that for a week straight now. At other times, I stared at the patterns on Zeeshan's bedsheets, for a guy who looked so masculine, he used floral bedsheets with purple and green flowers, and I found it fascinating. Why'd anyone paint flowers green? My mattress had an indentation on it from me lying on it 14 hours a day. My lifestyle and daily life behaviour patterns started worrying my friends. They were scaring me.

Zeeshan was too worried. I honestly thought that he was worried because he caught me staring at his bedsheets when he woke up beyond midnight a few days back. This one day when I had been staring at my cobwebs (yes, mine, I had grown fond of it), Zeeshan crept onto my bed and sat on the edge. He looked at me and then looked at what I was staring at and said, '*Bhai*, why don't you find something that motivates you to get out of bed? There has to be something. Anything that makes you want to make a move in the morning.' I took a minute to think and looked at him. Zeeshan was staring at my cobwebs as well. I reply, 'Bro, I think I haven't had breakfast for a week now.' Zeeshan turned to me and said, 'Perfect, you are going to wake up every day at 9 am to eat breakfast. The breakfast will be your motivation!' And that is how my new routine, my new lifestyle had begun. Now I got up, ate my breakfast, slept, ate my lunch, slept again, ate my dinner and slept again. When I was awake and not eating, I sang. My song of choice? The evergreen song, *Sach keh raha hai deewana*. There was never a better song to nurse a broken heart. I serenaded it fourteen times a day at the top of my voice, playing with my headphones on Zeeshan's old phone. I think he regretted lending me his phone on the second day because while I was serenading, everyone else was suffering with my off-tune Scream Queen version. By day 5, it was still questionable if Vivaan pitied me or got tired of my screeching, but he'd always bring me food to cheer me up. Zeeshan looked at Vivaan and put the food in my hand. Both of them went off to sleep early that night. My new routine had become a lot of people's new routine. We were Mahjong tiles stacked against one another, and I had long fallen off the table. I was Devdas, and Vivaan and Zeeshan were my Chunni Babu. And like all Devdas, I got drunk and when bottles opened, no one drank alone in our room. So we would pick our corners and start singing at the top of our voices, no speakers, no music, just us and the clinking of the bottles against the floor, *Maar daaala, Maar daala.* After fifteen minutes of our screaming competition because apparently, someone mentioned that the one with the loudest voice had the biggest heartbreak, Yash rushed out of his room and came into ours. '*Bhai*, I jumped out of bed because I thought someone was beating dogs on campus.' We glared at him, and I raised my half-filled glass to him. He took it and sat with us on the ground. '*Bhai bardasht nhi kar sakta hai toh peeta kyun hai?'* (Why do you drink if you can't handle it?) I snatched my glass back from him and tried to look at my reflection on it in the dimmed light. Realising it was pointless, I looked towards him and squinted my eyes and said, *'Kaun kambakhat bardasht karne ke liye peeta hai. Hum toh peete hai ki yahaan baith sake, tumhe bardasht kr sake, Afreen ko bhula sake.'* (Which wretched soul drinks to tolerate, I drink so that I can sit here so that you can tolerate me so that I can forget Afreen.) I lit a cigarette and every puff I inhaled was accompanied by an alternative, 'She loves me, she loves me not.' In the end, I snuffed it out with a 'she loves me'. Vivaan looked at the butt and said with tearing eyes, *'Bhai, ek kash aur tha. Akhri cigarette thi!'* (Bro, there was one more puff left. It was the last cigarette!) Yash had had enough of our Devdas and Chunni Babu episodes and made the conscious choice to dive into the role of 'I can fix him – Chandramukhi'. And by whatever means necessary he worked his magic with Vivaan and Zeeshan, and I was the target. He came up with a plan to save me. I'll let you all judge if this was revenge or the last resort. I was going to be hit on my balls every time I took Afreen's name. Have you

5. 5

ever felt as if the world had paused and there was this ringing inside your head, and your ears and when you were back to the coherent world, you had to reorient yourself with your existence? 4 times. I felt my soul leave my body. I risked the possibility of never having kids 4 times. But as we say, every dog has his day, Yash accidentally mentioned the name of 'She-who-must-not-be-named' and I got to sack him in the nuts, and he immediately dropped the 'no name' penalty. I had a smile on my face the whole day. This wasn't easy. Afreen had left the college; her internship was over. But I was so closely associated with her that I couldn't accept or let people know she had left, not just the college but also my life. I ignored calls from home, stayed alone, and stayed awake all night. I couldn't handle it anymore. I thought maybe I should seek help. The biggest irony is that medical students don't want to have a check-up at their own college hospital because they fear being judged. They don't want to become another case study or a protagonist in their professor's stories. So I decided to seek online counselling. I Googled some good counsellors, made a list, and even connected with a few. But I wasn't satisfied. I already knew their advice: 'Don't do this, wake up early, eat well, let it go and blah, blah, blah.' I tried seeking help from my parents, but their advice was straightforward: 'Focus on your studies. These things happen.' They were right, but I wasn't mature enough to understand their words at the time. I needed conversations; I needed someone to say, 'I know you're hurt, but I'm with you; you'll get through this.' I was losing hope, and what do you do when you lose hope? You scroll through your gallery, finding and living all those good moments of your past again. The highlights of the photos showed my White Coat ceremony-day pictures, a memorable day indeed. The day we received our white coat for the first time. This was followed by lunch. A short clip from that day also surfaced on my mobile screen, and it was a speech by our Professor of Psychiatry, Dr. Dhawan. I had never heard someone as diligently as I had listened to Dr. Dhawan that day. Why not him? Why couldn't he be my counsellor? After comparing the pros and cons, I decided to visit his OPD the next day. I chose 1:45 pm because the closing time of the OPD was 2. It was usually the time when there were no patients or just a few ones getting their reports checked. My plan was to pass by the OPD and get a side view to check if anyone else was there. To my disappointment, there were three patients in the queue. Feeling more anxious than usual, I turned back and started walking fast.

To label Dr. Dhawan as just a psychiatrist would be an understatement. He was a guide and a friend for all of us. Often in psychiatry, labels are used to identify patients. But, he considered accepting people the way they were. His presence in the psychiatric world was a paradox. Despite judgements being the basis of understanding issues in the world of medicine, he preferred to remain non-judgmental. People adored him as a psychiatrist because they could simply exist as who they were around him. His strength was to listen to his patients without imposing his judgments upon them. He usually never interrupted his patients while they were speaking. His patients felt that they were not being defined by their sufferings. He didn't offer any 'grand solutions', instead his approach was of 'unconditional acceptance'. The goal was not just to treat patients but also to accompany them through tough times. He would often ask his patients to recommend him a book, a song or just paint a picture centered on the life they were leading. He believed that art is a means to express our emotions and a tool for healing. People who had difficulty articulating their feelings verbally, often found this very helpful. Also, engaging in creative activities was a stress reliever. Through art, we get to explore aspects of our own self which are otherwise hidden.

Dr. Dhawan was known for his calm demeanour and deep empathy. As a psychiatrist with years of experience, he'd seen a variety of patients from all walks of life. One of the most challenging cases he had counselled was Dr. Naina's. We got to know about his encounter with Dr. Naina through Dr. Naina herself. One fine day, when she was teaching us during our ward duty, she narrated how Dr. Dhawan's counselling sessions were helping her deal with the toxicity in the department.

When Dr. Naina first visited Dr. Dhawan, she was carrying the weight of a thousand unspoken thoughts. She explained to Dr. Dhawan that she had been thinking about quitting residency. She endured too much work pressure, and she couldn't handle it. Dr. Naina mentioned that she felt she was in a very toxic workplace environment. There was constant competition, and the seniors were treating the residents just as tools to get any work done. It made her feel small and invisible. There was a complete lack of work-life balance. Dr. Dhawan realised her issue and said that he understood how the toxic environment was draining the passion she had once felt for her field of work.

Dr. Naina agreed that she initially enjoyed helping other women in their most difficult times, but now it all felt like just a duty.

Dr. Dhawan explained, 'It's completely okay to prioritise mental health and well-being. You're not a failure for doing this. It is actually a form of strength.' He added, 'Only you define your own success and failure.'

Dr. Naina said, 'I can't remember the last time I did something for myself. I don't know whether quitting is a sign of weakness or if I'm just being realistic.'

Dr. Dhawan replied, 'Residency is a demanding field, but it is also a time for the development of compassionate and competent physicians. You need to focus on what truly matters to you in this moment.'

Dr. Naina said, 'But I still want to help people. I don't want to be judged.'

Dr. Dhawan said, 'I know there are a lot of issues, but I also appreciate that despite all these issues, you continue to care for your patients.' He advised, 'You should focus more on the process, rather than just the outcome. You can't change the pace of residency, but you can change your approach. Change your relationship with your expectations.' He added, 'And yes, I know Dr. Ghosh. I know things are difficult in your department. Many residents have approached me regarding this, and I'm in talks with the administration to address it. They need to do something about it.'

Dr. Naina said that she didn't receive a solution that day, but from that moment on, she continued to ponder her choice and what she must do. The decision was hers to make. The decision now didn't feel like a burden but like a possibility. She added that Dr. Dhawan had encountered many residents with similar situations in the past—those who faced overwhelming stress and thought about quitting their careers. However, after his counselling sessions, all of them continued their residencies.

After my failed attempts to meet Dr. Dhawan during OPD hours, I decided that maybe it was not in my destiny to meet him. But destiny can change forever with one last try. I decided to visit his OPD again next week. But this time, in the early morning hours. I needed to sleep as I hadn't been able to sleep for the last couple of days. I bought the OPD ticket which I refused to buy earlier since I didn't want my name to be registered in the patient section of the same hospital I studied at, but maybe buying the OPD ticket showed my intent to seek help. I got in line outside the OPD alongside other patients, and when I was finally called in, I started feeling anxious. My legs were shaking. However, I wanted to experience going through the process. I wanted to know why this guy was so famous, although I was scared of being diagnosed with some serious condition considering my conduct in the past few weeks. I entered the room wearing my apron because I had my practicals scheduled in the evening. As I entered, I was greeted by Dr. Dhawan. 'Oh, young man, what happened, a victim of your own profession *ya dil ke mareez ho*, and why didn't you visit all those days when you were just sneaking around my chamber from outside?

I said, 'So you noticed?' 'Why didn't you call me?'

'Oh, I wanted to contact you, even asked the nursing staff to let me know when you are here, but I guess you always were in such a hurry. So, have a seat, what brings you here my boy?'

'Oh and could you wait for just ten minutes, I need to feed Captain Nemo, so I'll be quick.'

Suddenly, I wasn't sure if I was seeking help from the right person. His priority was his own life, which I understand should be, but hey, I am here, right in front of you. A person who hasn't slept for the last four days and do you even care? Meanwhile, I gave a quick look at his OPD Chamber. You try to find out about a person by the things he associates himself with. I saw only one book on his table. From a distance, I could see there was a long-haired man painted on that book. My curiosity led me to get up to have a better look at this book. It was titled 'Autobiography of a Yogi' by Parmahansa Yogananda. The walls in his chamber were painted a muted pink colour with an off-white ceiling.

After a few minutes, Dr. Dhawan returned to his chamber. He asked if I had lunch. I said, 'Yes'. Although I was very hungry. My stomach was rumbling loudly from hunger, but at that moment, I wanted to get things over with first.

I told him everything—how I tried to follow a routine and go to the gym, but nothing made me happy. I felt lonely even around friends. He didn't say a word; he just listened, the more he avoided interrupting, the more I was getting comfortable and the more I could reveal. He looked at me for some time and finally said, 'What do you like to do?' 'You're not doing what you love, Jai. You're doing what you've taken from others. You're trying to impose things on yourself that you think will make you feel loved, appreciated.'

'Well, I remember a boy who used to have a camera and make videos all day. I recall how you used to roam around just to get the best shot. I'm sure you must have loved that stress because that stress also ensured satisfaction at the end of the day. So, my friend, do what you like, what you think brings you satisfaction. As long as you're trying to prove something to someone, you're not free.'

He also mentioned a subject called theosophy, saying it's interesting but he didn't want me to delve into it just yet; we could discuss it another time, maybe in our next session.

I learned from Dr. Dhawan's counselling sessions that words can either heal or break someone. He emphasised that with good friends, the journey through medical school will be smoother.

'We are kind and forgiving to strangers, but when it comes to our own friends, we belittle them, and take them for granted. Kindness begins with yourself. We forgive so much in relationships, so why not in friendships? Lack of appreciation can ruin even the most beautiful long-term bonds. There's no guarantee you'll get the same response from everyone. Sometimes, despite your best efforts, you'll fail and start doubting yourself. But my friend, that's life.

Even my crush hasn't accepted my friend request yet, even though she knows I'm the famous Dr. Dhawan today. I think she's here to keep me humble whenever I start to get arrogant. But whenever I count my blessings and my problems, my blessings always outweigh my problems.'

For the next few days, I had more sessions with Dr. Dhawan. He mostly listened and used to say a few lines at the end. I basically started to understand his methods. I realised most of our problems or things that we perceive as a problem are basically because we lack confidence. What Dr. Dhawan made sure of was that I didn't feel any different. I feel we start to lack belief in our abilities when bad things happen, and what we need is just some hope and words of encouragement from the person we trust.

Life was slowly inching towards normalcy. I got myself a new phone. My mum made my sister call me and I could hear Dad talking in the background. '*Bhaiya*, Mom made *tinday* again today.' I laughed and said, '*Tindays* are okay.' It was the weekend and we were done drinking inside our room. Have you ever watched a ray of sunshine pierce through a small gap in the blinds? We needed a ray of sunshine. So Zeeshan, Vivaan and I made a spontaneous decision to go on a high trip to Goa. Now, if you've ever been to Goa, with its pretty beaches, blue skies, salty air and coconut tree-lined roads which call you to go on drives, and rides and never reach a destination, renting your vehicle of choice is the go-to there and you must have a driver's license and you must not at all take the vehicle out of the designated area permitted to it. We took our rented car and enjoyed the road and the air and the unwinding of our tangled affairs. We were chasing the sunshine. We were feeling the wind on our faces and went to Belgaum, crossing the border without even realising it. Now I know bad decisions, but bad luck that I never even signed up for! Yes, I know that too. I have expertise in it. The car wasn't supposed to go out of Goa and it definitely wasn't supposed to be in Belgaum which is infamous for selling stolen cars. The car had a tracker which the rental service had used to track us entering into Belgaum and that led to them believing that we were stealing the car. And to top it off, there was a car which had been racing with us for the past 50 km and we were winning. The adrenaline had Vivaan craving for a cigarette because a 'celebratory smoke' was needed, and he was bored of racing. We spotted a shop and decided to get off and get a smoke. But as soon as Vivaan got out of the car, someone pushed him into a car which I then realised was the same one racing with us. I was sitting inside the car with my head poking out thinking what just happened. I asked Zeeshan, 'Yaar, if they can't handle losing, why compete?' Zeeshan, *'Bhai! Vivaan ko bujha denge woh log* (Bro! They will hurt Vivaan.). We need to help him.' I took off my shoes, picked one each in my hands and said, 'Let's go!' As soon as I stepped out of the car, I fell face down. But my spirit for saving my friend wasn't down. I handed a shoe to Zeeshan and said, *'Khopdi tod saale ki'* (Break his forehead.). It also wasn't unsurprising when Zeeshan staggered close to the car with my shoe swinging in his hands, and instead of smashing skulls, he was smashed inside the car right beside Vivaan. Zeeshan, *'Bhai,* we need to help him.' I took off my shoes and picked each one in my hands as if they were bricks and said, 'Let's go.' But as soon as we stepped out, I fell down and the next thing I knew, Zeeshan and I were being stuffed inside the same car. Vivaan continued to ask for a cigarette banging his hands on the car windows. We felt like we were being kidnapped and realised it was possible that our last visual of Vivaan would be of him asking for a cigarette from us which we couldn't even fulfil. Surprisingly enough, we ended up in a police station ten minutes later, completely clueless but still relieved that we were saved. What was even weirder was that we were being made to sit with the criminals in a lock up when we were the victims! But since I was really high and still in a fun mood, I asked the criminals inside, '*Kya kiya?*'

Criminal 1: '*Chain kheecha* (Pulled the chain).'

 Criminal 2: 'Killed my ex.'

And that is when the police inspector came and asked us, '*Gaadi kyun churai?*' (Why did you steal the car?) I looked at the criminals and said, '*Humne gaadi churai?* ' (Did we steal the car?) Then as if I could see the cogwheels turning in my head, I looked at my friends, then at the inspector and then at myself, '*Humne gaadi kab churai?*' (When did we steal the car?) An hour later, with two impressed criminals, countless 'I am sorry', and Rs. 10000 short, we finally managed out of the police station. Vivaan, '*Bhai*, cigarette?' Zeeshan, 'Jai, buy him a packet.' Vivaan finally had his cigarette and we headed back.

On a random Thursday morning, Zeeshan while scrolling on his phone chimed, 'I found a new girl for you.' I was sprawled on my bed smoking Vivaan's unfinished joint from last night and said, 'Leave me alone, you won't find true love again.' 'Zeeshan, this is all a lie, trust me, you will find love again.'

I was thirsty and looked around for water and finally crawled out of the bed to fill the water bottle on my bedside. Zeeshan looked up at me and handed me his bottle with a sleazy smile. *Scoundrel!* Running two flights of stairs and with two filled water bottles, I walked back to my room.

My love life was barren but it was finally spring for others and some people had a tropical forest in their backyard. Harshil and Chaavi decided to share their marrow subscription. They paid equally for the subscription and with the rest of the money they planned a holiday trip to Goa. Meanwhile, I realised that cigarettes and all other addictions give you momentary pleasure. Once you find out what gives you true and lifelong happiness, none of those addictions will be required, and I remembered that my purpose of joining the college was to become a doctor so I had to work hard to be a good one. So, I started studying for my final year. I used to study all day while my friends had one additional job along with studying and that was to search for a girl for me. Every junior was committed. Vivaan and I had these sessions of 'Theories of Life' while studying. Vivaan, 'We are alpha males, bro. We don't go and find out girls. They come looking for us. We hit the gym, we make money, and we don't cry like babies.' Oh, and did I mention that this was the same guy who was crying yesterday night because he lost his crush in class fourth? Their bond was about sharing their lunchboxes. He didn't even lose her; she just shifted to another school. He said that he never felt so comfortable around any friend after her. He added, 'Nobody was as enthusiastic to share, and nobody waited till I finished my lunch.' Some memories stay with us for life, till the very end. My sessions with Dr. Dhawan changed my perspective on a lot of things. A great teacher teaches you gratitude. You realise that true love is in giving and not demanding. After my pre-final year, I got to connect with Aadarsh again. Owing to the success of my short film, I was appointed Secretary of the Cultural Committee, while he was heading the Editorial board of the college. I remember us having differences in our way of seeing life. I believed in 'One life, live it', whereas he believed in 'Live wisely, think long term'. We used to plan events together. He often used to suggest that more people should get to listen to our conversations. I used to say, 'Maybe someday.'

This was after my pre-final exams. I was finally healing. Going to have food alone in the mess was not an awkward situation anymore. I didn't feel like I had to drag myself to attend lectures. The feeling of heaviness and unease was no longer there. I started going to the library after my classes. My goal was to be there for a few hours daily, just sit and try to focus even if I was not able to perform at my optimum capacity. Eating in the library was strictly prohibited but right from the beginning, I was not good at following rules, so I brought my favourite dark chocolate with me. Did I mention that I hated eating dark chocolate when I frist started college? It was Afreen who loved it and being with her I became a fan too. So one Saturday, the second half of our classes was over and I decided to go to the library. Luckily I had one piece of chocolate left in the pocket of my apron. I took the last seat facing the library. Most of the students preferred the last seat but facing the wall, but my curious mind always wanted to know what was happening with everyone around, which book they were reading, what colour of a highlighter they were using, and why the couple who used to sit together every day was sitting at different places today. So I arranged my books on the desk, clicked an aesthetic photograph of my presence in the library and shared it on Snapchat so that everyone knew 'Jai attends library now' and my streak continued. I took out the dark chocolate from my pocket and to my disappointment, it had melted. Initially, I thought of putting it back but who cares, let me get my hands dirty. The chief librarian was sitting at the front entrance desk of the library, and from this distance, you couldn't correctly assume whether he was watching you or he was asleep because, in both conditions, his head was affixed towards you. So I had to open my chocolate under my desk and to eat it, I had to bring my head down to the height of my tab so that I was not caught. To be honest, I was pretty successful at my job, but I didn't realise that a girl was sitting in the opposite row on the cornermost side. She was observing my activity. Maybe the noise from the chocolate wrapper was disturbing her, or maybe she wanted my chocolate. You are so confused when a nerd gives you looks. So, the name of this nerd was

5. 5

Natasha. She was very shy, an introvert, and one of the top rankers of our batch. So with an uncomfortable smile, I put the leftover pieces of the chocolate back into my pocket and licked the chocolate stick over my fingers. She gaped and I was finally there with an apologetic grin.

Natasha and I started to share the same corner of the library after that day. She didn't utter a word nor did I for days. Perhaps a person might not seem good to you at first, but with time, their presence starts to feel comforting. Our exam schedule was announced next week. So I requested her to guide me with my studies, and we arrived at a mutual agreement. She would teach me all the main subjects, and I would teach her all the short subjects, considering my situation with my studies. She didn't want me to go with the main subjects as that could ruin her preparation as well. She had a habit of murmuring when she used to study, whereas I liked a quiet atmosphere for studies, so I thought maybe the next day I would ask her to be quiet but to my surprise, there was no murmuring. In fact, it never happened after that. It took me a while to realise that the people who really care for you know what makes you feel comfortable around them. Love is about giving. When you stop putting in efforts, love doesn't feel like a strength to you. There were days when I used to skip going to the library or she was not present. Initially, it made me feel anxious. I thought she might get a new study partner but she didn't. She used to wait, and after you have failed in past relationships, how soothing it is for you when someone just waits and listens to you, and you speak without fear of judgement, without interruptions. With time, we got close, and we didn't talk about that, but there were symptoms. We were chatting on WhatsApp although we were sitting next to each other in the library. We decided together what to eat after study sessions, and we bitched about our colleagues together. I thought maybe I should ask her for a coffee date outside the campus, but I thought why not cook the world-famous, *Jev Pasta Arabiata*. This was a pasta dish that I invented which was nothing but pasta with a lot of mozzarella cheese and even named it similar to my name so that people who eat it could know its glorious origins.

So I planned to cook for Natasha on the weekend. I invited her to my place. I didn't realise that she would join me early before lunchtime. She brought some drinks and my favourite mozzarella cheese. I was delighted to have help with cooking, but soon I was disappointed. When I cook, I am the ruler of the kitchen and anyone else feels like a total invader. Cooking should be a solitary activity (if you wish to cook well). I asked her to simply sit and wait for the food to be served. Maybe I shouldn't have said that because I received no compliments for the pasta I cooked.

Amidst all these things, we continued our studies. So one day, while I was preparing to go to my study session with Natasha, she came into my room, jumped on me and directly started kissing me and just when we were proceeding further, I woke up and found out that I had been hugging Baileys and Love Volume 1. I got out of bed and sat down to study. Way to go!

Yash casually came to my room to check how far along I had gotten, as I had just recently started studying and there was a lot of portion.

Yash: 'How much study is left?'

I replied, 'Cardio.....Cardio, Respi, Endo......Cardio, Respi, Endo, GIT...........Cardio, Respi, Endo, GIT, Labour, Paediatrics, Orthopaedic, Radio.......'

'Keep going brother, you are almost done!'. Yash said, '*Bhai, from the first year to final year studies have increased exponentially, but ironically lecture class attendance has decreased exponentially.*' Everybody had gone home for Diwali, but only Yash and I stayed for lectures. Staying back at the hostel on holidays was a very odd experience, the whole college gave you holiday vibes, the canteen was closed, the mess was closed, nearby shops around the college were closed, and the weather seemed more intense to you on those days if it was raining, it rained cats and dogs, if it's summer, there is scorching heat, actually there is nothing special about the weather those days. It's just that when you have few distractions in your life, you observe nature very meticulously. After lectures, Yash and I went out to have some food. Yash saw a dog and tried to pet him. She didn't like it. He got bitten. Zeeshan called me and said, 'Bro, this world is so unfair to kind people.'

'You should have avoided going there,' I said.

I went to the owner and asked him whether the dog was vaccinated. We got into a conversation and I shared some tips with him on how to train dogs! Yash screamed, 'Asshole, first take me to the hospital.' I took him to casualty at our college. There was a first-year junior resident on duty, and I told him the entire incident and asked him to give vaccination for rabies. He looked at both of us and then excused himself. I followed after him thinking he went to ask a nurse about the vaccine but instead, I witnessed the resident googling the regimen. That scared me but I didn't tell Yash about it. He gave the injection and asked to come for follow-up as per the googled regime 0, 3, 7, 14, and 28 days!

One evening, Vivaan, Zeeshan, and I sat on the rooftop of the boys' hostel. Though I had developed a good bond with Natasha, we were still officially not in a relationship. I preferred to stay alone in my room, hesitant to ask my friends for company. Somehow, they sensed I needed company and stayed with me most of the time.

Breaking the silence we had shared for over an hour, Vivaan said, 'Jai, do you know a girl from Delhi who joined in the first year? She's incredibly beautiful, and the whole college is after her, but I'm sure my brother will win her over.'

Zeeshan added, 'Yeah, I saw her today leaving the lecture hall. She's amazing, buddy.'

5. 5

After sipping another glass of rum, I asked, 'What's her name?'

Vivaan replied, 'Isha.'

He continued, 'Let's go tomorrow, and wait outside the lecture hall. It's been just 15 days since she has arrived; no one must have approached her yet.'

Later that night, I got her Instagram ID from Yash, which also confirmed her beauty. Uncertain about my situation with Natasha, I thought this might be a second chance, and she could be the one.

The next day, I and my friends waited for Isha outside the lecture hall. When the lecture ended, I became anxious, avoiding the main exit. As Isha approached, she waved in our direction, and I thought she recognised me from the Instagram follow request. However, her eyes were searching for someone behind us.

That someone was Aadarsh, my immediate junior in college. At that moment, I just wanted to punch him in the face and break his nasal bone, but I couldn't. I just felt helpless.

Frustrated, I turned to Zeeshan and then to Vivaan, muttering, 'Friends like you shouldn't exist.'

5. 5

Life was certainly not a bowl full of cherries. Upon return to the hostel, I went to Appa's room. There I saw a fish in the tank, thinking it was hungry, and gave extra food to the fish. The fish died. Appa Sir got emotional.

So after fucking up my life pretty good I decided to do the right thing now: 'Funeral of the fish'.

Appa Sir, '*Itni choti si umar main chodke chali gayi mujhe.*' (She left us at such a tender age.)

Zeeshan said, '*Waise humara zyada interaction nahi hua hai* (Although we didn't have much interaction) but you seemed like a good swimmer. We will miss you.'

I stood in awkward silence and then said, 'Goldfish is one of the most commonly domesticated fish. It has a speed of 1.37 kmph and lives for fifteen years.'

Zeeshan then whispered into my ears to shut down Google and stand in silence.

CHAPTER 6

THE PRESSURE TEST

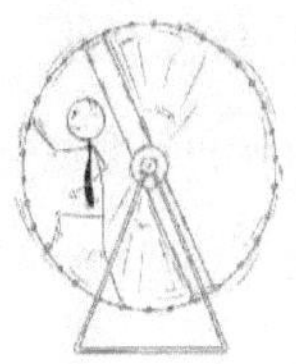

As we got closer to final exams, stress increased and everybody had their own ways of dealing with stress. Zeeshan increased his repetitions and set to deal with the stress. Sometimes I felt that he would knock the examiners out if he didn't know the answer. Books were always in the hands of students as they walked to the bus, on the bus, at the centre, and even entering the exam hall. It was only then they realised it was cheating, so they kept the books back in the bags and went to take the exam. There were no pouches; all the stationary was carried in our hands, along with the hall ticket. Yash taught us 20 hostilities 'NRP' (*Neonatal Resuscitation Program*) as no one had studied one day before the exam.

5. 5

Vivaan had a meditation room in the hostel in which everybody came to relax, by smoking a joint. Vivaan said, 'Inhale the greenery, and exhale the crap! To all of us disciples who love his therapy after exams.'

(ROOM TEMPLATE: GO GREEN)

Einstein's time travel theory: Einstein decided to have a party at his home, and for that, he printed an advertisement in the newspaper! Nobody from the future arrived, so time travel is not possible! So, we had our practicals from the next day and we were slumped doing revisions and accepted that whatever would happen, would happen. And we just thought, *bas ye waqt guzar jaye.* (This time somehow passes away.)

Apart from hard work, final-year practicals also depended on luck. There were many things that were not in our control like the mood of our examiner and the patient we got. From an exam point of view, there were 2 types of patients.

Patient 1: Not cooperating, tells different history to students and different history to the examiner.

Patient 2: Sweetest, tells everything that has to be written in the exam paper.

5. 5

The most dreaded subject for practicals in the final year was Pediatrics because the duration of grand viva used to make us queasy.

Medicine was easy to deal with unless you land up getting a CNS case because after getting a CNS case you suffer Transient Global Amnesia.

In surgery, everyone demanded an appendix case for history taking. The head staff of the department got annoyed by this and introduced a chit system. Along with surgery, we also had viva for Orthopaedics. We were asked to identify X-rays, bones and instruments. All this certainly resulted in increased sympathetic activity in our bodies.

A group of hostilities were planning to go on a trek in cars and bikes. I had already booked a seat in the car knowing that the trip was going to be long. However, Subhramanyam arrived early and took my seat. When I protested, Subhramanyam said, 'If cheating happens in the game, then I won't play. I am going now.' I was unhappy with his ruthless behaviour, but my words fell on deaf ears. So, I had to ride the bike, which was not a good experience. I learned that you couldn't reserve your space, you had to occupy it as this buffoon did.

During the trek, I got separated and lost from the group. My friends searched for me, but I had no clue that they would get so worried. The villagers also scared them by saying, 'Many people fall here.' They were all extremely stressed. Eventually, they found me standing with a villager. However, instead of relief, they started screaming at me, 'We have been searching for you for so long, don't you understand?' I didn't understand the severity of the situation and replied, 'You were looking for me, and I was waiting for you here!'

Unfortunately, my response only made them angrier, and they started cursing me. Even the villagers joined in the screaming. I wanted to argue back, but I knew it would only make things worse.

We headed back to the hostel, with Subhramanyam sitting in the centre seat of the car. I felt envious of him because I couldn't get my preferred seat, even though I had reserved one. However, I didn't blame anyone as I knew how much Subhramanyam cared about these things, and none of us dared to oppose him. Later that evening, we all dressed up and had dinner. At the end of our trip, we decided to gate crash a wedding but realised it was not the wedding that day, it was the *haldi ceremony*. I commented, 'This *haldi ceremony* looks like a chicken marinating ceremony.' But no one paid attention to me. They were all too busy finding food and deciding what to eat. Honestly, travelling in a group requires a lot of adjustment. It is successful only if you are ready to take care of each other, and agree to the budget set because we all have a different notion around which we explore the world, to give each other freedom.

Many of my batchmates who had taken a drop the year were joining me later at my college as my juniors. Saying that they didn't deserve it wouldn't be fair. I was lucky enough to be supported by my parents in my very first attempt which helped me enter a medical college. A call from a friend seeking a bone set for 4000 bucks initially had me in doubt but later I agreed as his parents were my neighbours back in Pune.

We had a culture at our hostel to bid farewell to our seniors in the most unique way. For one whole day, they had to be

5. 5

in the role of our juniors and had to endure ragging. The farewell ritual for interns, funded by all but the interns themselves, culminated in a grand party. However, funds fell short of the desired alcohol quality and quantity, leading nine of us on a daring mission to Daman to procure cheaper alcohol. We all came back following different routes to avoid getting caught.

The interns arrived at the venue in luxury cars, while other batches arrived by bus. At the event, the final-year students presented two PowerPoint presentations: one highlighted their academic achievements and pride for the professors, while the other revealed the compilation of the seniors' mishaps over the years. The celebration featured a bonfire, weed, alcohol, and a thrilling treasure hunt leading to a surprise party on the terrace.

CHAPTER 7

UNSEEN TIMES

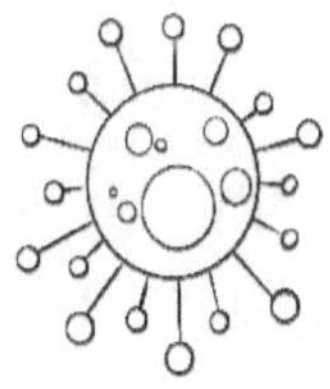

Medhavi had a mind which could be compared to a labyrinth- part memory,part fear and part invention, her batchmates say she's unwell but in her head everything makes sense.

But Medhavi, you need to understand that this can lead to the end of your friendship with Aarvi. Hasn't she been a good friend to you all these years? Mom didn't even call me today. She talks to my brother, Madhav every day. Nobody loves me. Marilyn Monroe died by suicide. The food at the mess today was so oily. I remember an episode of Crime Patrol where the staff mixes poison to loot customers. Nitin (her boyfriend) will harm me if I ever leave him, he said that day that he can't think of me being with someone else, why do boyfriends cheat, I think even Harshil and Chhavi will break up one day…..

Someone knocks on the door.

Medhavi?

Medhavi recognised this voice. This was Aarvi.

Aarvi is here to apologise to Medhavi for her misbehaviour with her this morning. Aarvi, her best friend had not submitted her proxy for the medicine lecture.

Medhavi quickly packed his chocolate box. She didn't realise that she had by now consumed thirty milk bars and hadn't changed her clothes after the second half of the classes.

'Hey, I am so sorry for today. I could have managed but Sir had very strict guidelines to not take any proxy calls. , Aarvi said, 'Sorry….you haven't changed yet?'

Hey, it's totally fine. I am not even thinking about it. Ya, I forgot to change. Actually, I had slept in the afternoon and woke up just fifteen minutes ago.

Mona Lisa's smile followed.

Aarvi: 'Thank god, I was so stressed. Now let's have dinner together.'

Medhavi: 'Sure, sure. You go and I will join you in ten.'

5. 5

Medhavi closed her door.

Samar got a proxy today in medicine class. Aarvi and Samar were laughing together today after the practicals. She used to wait for me whenever I used to tell her to go and eat first. Today she left. What have I done? Why do I have to feel all this?

Medhavi, unlike falling in love with someone special like in movies was trying to make love for herself first. It was not like she was a bad student. She scored decently and was involved in a lot of activities ranging from playing basketball to cultural events of the college. She even dated Dr. Ravindra, a new resident in the Department of Psychiatry of our college for a while, hoping that the field of medicine he belonged to might have shaped him into a gentleman who could understand her behaviour and frequent mood swings, but she was totally disappointed. On their second meeting, Dr. Ravindra invited her to dinner at his place. Medhavi decided to go. She had no idea that his other colleagues were also invited for the dinner that day. After a brief acquaintance with each other, they all sat for dinner where to the contrary expectations of Medhavi, they started to mimic how she used to talk and how she used to be overexcited about everything around her. One female friend of Ravindra joked about how she would react on her first night after marriage. They even asked her if she was mentally mature enough for a relationship. Medhavi was quiet. She knew that she had made the wrong choice. She didn't want to get hurt again. Everybody she met in the past had taken advantage of her situation. In college, most people of our age make a choice out of two options. First, you accept whatever happens to you because you fear if you speak against it, you will be left alone and the second one is that you take a stand for yourself, which is not easy for many, you get bullied, you are laughed at, and you sink into depression. Medhavi felt terrible. She wanted to cry, in fact, run away, but she didn't dare to do so. She smiled. She laughed along with them at jokes which were made on her only. That night, they all took a group photo post-dinner. Medhavi uploaded it to her Instagram story, the caption said, 'Family away from home'.

5.5

Later that week, we got to know about the pandemic having reached India and now there would be a complete lockdown. Our hospital was also going to be converted into a COVID care centre. Everybody was scared but we knew that if we all did our part, we would get through it. We all saw videos of donning and doffing the PPE kit as that was the most important and new thing in our lives. On campus, no one was allowed to play but was supposed to do duty! During these scary times, some of our friends and relatives would say, '*Ye COVID kuch hai kya ya fir sirf paise kamaane ke liye hai.*' (Is COVID even a real thing or is it just a hoax to extract money from people?) We had two phones inside the ward. We used to inform all relatives about the update of the patient every day. Sometimes, we used to get depressing videos of kids asking us to please leave their parents but unfortunately, we couldn't do anything about it.

COVID was not going anywhere soon and the long-duty hours in the uncomfortable PPEs were becoming a headache, so to lift our spirits we decided to make a motivational audio of all the inspirational stories of doctors in these difficult times.

1) DR. NAINA, JUNIOR RESIDENT, OBGY

At the beginning of the pandemic, I was part of the team which performed a caesarean section on a COVID-positive pregnant lady. She was the first COVID-positive pregnancy case in my city. The atmosphere in the operating room was that of panic and confusion. The disease was still new. We had limited knowledge of the treatment options and their severity. And to top it up, we had no clue about the effects of COVID on pregnancy. There were a lot of uncertainties regarding the outcome. Also, the treating doctors and healthcare staff feared the risk of contracting COVID. But, performing that C-section was the need of the hour to safeguard the well-being of that mother and her baby. I had conducted several deliveries and C-sections in the past, but this was a whole other ball game. With a thrill of dread and fear, I along with senior consultants, nurses, anaesthesiologists, paediatricians and other staff, entered the operating room with full PPE gear. The PPE was uncomfortable and the face shield fogged. Performing the surgery was a herculean task. But we managed to do it successfully. The mother and the baby recovered well and were sent home without any complications. This was one of

5. 5

the most challenging procedures that I performed so far. It was also one of my finest moments, an epitome of the Hippocratic Oath I took so many years ago.

2) MD DERMATOLOGY

These past 2 years have been really difficult for me because my family lives abroad and I haven't been able to meet them. Sometimes I would tell myself that it's all good only because I wouldn't want to give them any infections acquired from work. At least I know that they'll be safe when not with me. Although I am the third-generation doctor in my family, I initially wanted to become a Quantum physicist. I had taken my SATs at school and was all set to go abroad for higher studies. But I started watching Grey's Anatomy and surprisingly enough, that's what made me shift to medicine. It's strange where one can derive inspiration from. I mean, Sir Isaac Newton discovered gravity when he was a teenager. It's not that he didn't know that if you jump, you'll come down —it was the falling of an apple which gave him an epiphany. Never look down upon any experience as silly or shallow. It might just change your entire life. One thing that this pandemic taught me though was that life is uncertain. You don't know if you'll even live tomorrow. Anything can change in an instant. So, live every day like it's your last day. Pursue all those hobbies that you've always wanted to, learn the skill which you couldn't earlier due to studies, watch that movie which you've been delaying, and enjoy today.

3) MD RESPIRATORY MEDICINE

At 3 am, a tired respiratory ward resident takes off his PPE after 12 hours. Drenched in sweat, he struggles to breathe under the N95+ surgical mask. He tries to stop his eyelids drooping, while he longs to sleep. He sits at the table, documenting, checking investigation reports, reviewing treatment plans and waiting for the time to pass until his colleague resting in the next room takes over and relieves him of the duty.

4) NURSE

I remember how excited I was for my first emergency night posting. All that time spent studying, nights agonising over papers, studying for finals, the all-over body rash that I developed 2 weeks before the end of my program because of stress – all of it was finally going to pay off. As excited as I was, fear and self-doubt began to creep in. I was finally on my own and I was terrified. I regretted not asking enough questions, not ordering the right tests, and saying something that would make me look dumb. For anyone who may be going through the same thing, you are not alone. It's completely normal to feel this way. Confidence takes time to build. You can buy the fanciest clothes, and the latest gadgets, and fake it until you make it, but those things won't really do much. It really just takes time and repetition. Take it one day at a time. Embrace your wins. You got this!

5) FOREIGN MEDICAL GRADUATE (FMG)

This year, a lot of things happened in the medical community. Doctors were beaten up, overworked, ill-treated and whatnot. But I want to point out the positive side of the Indian medical community, the community that gracefully rose to the challenge in these dire circumstances. First of all, the Studygram community has been so welcoming, informative and supportive. When doctors were being treated badly, many of them spoke up about it. They did their bit by holding healthy conversations and trying to spread awareness about violence against doctors. Secondly, as an Indian medical student studying in Russia, I always thought that FMGs are misunderstood, judged and tagged 'incompetent' doctors. But the support I've received from my fellow medicos has been overwhelming! It made me believe that not getting a government seat isn't the end of my career. Lastly, when the COVID wave hit India, apart from working in the frontline, doctors with any kind of social media presence provided free check-ups, online guidance, spread awareness, etc. We survived Mucormycosis, overworking, lack of beds and more, without giving up. So, if any premedical student is in doubt or rethinking their decision to pursue medicine, I would like to tell you that the medical fraternity stands together and welcomes them with open arms! Do not be afraid to pursue your dream.

6) MD INTERNAL MEDICINE

Internal medicine residency is tough, they say, but no one tells you why. It is not just the crazy hours, the patient load and studying that make it tough, it is much more than that. Residency teaches you about life and death. Be careful, this is about to get dark. No one teaches you how to deal with death, especially in MBBS. But as a resident, you're suddenly held accountable for someone's death! The contrast is immense, irrespective of whose fault it is, and I was crushed under it in my first week of residency. Luckily for me, the patient's relatives were kind enough to thank my colleagues and me for all the help, but that's not always the case, especially during COVID-19, when all doctors were subjected to death, at a very large number. It took a toll on us. I went through phases of denial, self-blame and to the point where I lost confidence in myself. I wanted to quit. But just talking to my friends and family helped me through it and that's how today, I stand where I am. The idea of death still brings me down and dealing with death needs to be taught in medical curriculum. To all those reading this, don't be scared to ask for help, don't blame yourself, and it is absolutely okay to take a break. You can't save the world unless you save yourself!

In this chaos, a ray of hope had come for all of us. The vaccination for COVID-19 was now available for everybody.

These were the common scenes I witnessed. I came to realise that this pandemic had hit every person on the planet hard. Many lost lives, many more lost livelihoods, and fear gripped everyone. Nobody asked us healthcare workers, how we were doing. All we did was take care of everyone but ourselves. Many of us were thrown out of our rented homes. We were sometimes even denied the essentials. I saw interns and residents gobbling their food in just two minutes. Sometimes they were surviving merely on water, waking up in the middle of the night to see if the monitors were still beeping, checking vitals, and to top it off, being criticised and abused by patient's relatives. COVID taught us something, gratitude and unconditional hope. It taught us to thrive, not just survive. I remember a patient who was admitted to the ICU for 46+ days, after which he was put on a non-invasive ventilator. During his stay, I was a mute spectator for the most part. His 27-year-old son visited him every day. He risked coming to the hospital every day, hoping that his father would get back up on his feet. His faith boosted the old man's will to live. A father himself sent his little daughter to her maternal grandparents so as to not infect her. He felt helpless. I saw a breadwinner succumbing to the illness. So many families were torn apart and scarred. We're at war with an invisible enemy. All we could do was hope, and being in the medical fraternity, we thought and decided, 'Let's try and be the guiding light to the people navigating through a dark and twisted tunnel. '

We all have seen kids crying to take injections but it was amusing for me to see a very well-built guy shutting his eyes scared of taking an injection. After vaccination, patients were made to sit in an observation room for *30* minutes, which seemed like another jail created by COVID-19. They got bored and made up different questions just to utilise the doctor in the room!

We got shocking news that Dr. Basu, our beloved Professor of Anatomy, died due to COVID. We were recalling how Dr. Basu used to boost our morale before our Anatomy practicals. His last blog when he was admitted to critical care was a quote by a Welsh poet, Dylan Thomas:

'Do not go gentle into that good night. Old age should burn and rave at the close of day; rage, rage against the dying of the light.' In these lines, Dylan Thomas is urging

individuals not to passively accept death, especially in old age. He encourages them to resist and fight against the fading away of life. Dr. Basu was always available for doubt sessions and poured his heart into making students understand human anatomy. His students who were now themselves doctors lent support from all over India, finding better options for his treatment, but failure was the outcome. Our college announced a scholarship in his name for students who score distinction marks in Anatomy. It was his last year in service before retirement, and he was going to live a happily retired life. He must be saving for forty years of his service period to finally enjoy probably his last decade of life but we don't decide when we die. COVID-19 seemed like an out-of-syllabus question in our lives much like those unexpected questions in our university papers, which feel as though they are meant to fail us and they do. Those who pass ride on good luck.

CHAPTER 8

THE POISONED WELL

About six months ago, during our posting in the Obstetrics and Gynaecology department, our group was leaving the ward early on a Saturday when a nurse informed us that Dr. Mitali Ghosh (Head of the Department of OBGY) wanted to see us. Despite being disappointed about missing lunch at Sorbbs' invitation, we reluctantly headed upstairs.

Upon entering the room, we found all the postgraduate students encircling a table where Ma'am was seated, flanked by Dr. Naina and Dr. Tanvi. The Head Ma'am invited us forward, introducing Dr. Naina and asking her to repeat her introduction. Dr. Naina, standing with tears streaming down her face, hesitated but eventually admitted, her voice fumbling, 'My name is Dr. Naina and I ki......my patients.....'

5. 5

'Louder Heroine, louder!!', said Dr. Ghosh.

Dr. Naina repeated the statement. This time, with her eyes affixed to the ground, her voice had gained courage.

She was louder than needed, she continued

'My Name is Dr. Naina and I quit.'

As Dr. Naina uttered this statement, she collapsed. The situation seemed dire, but the Head Ma'am dismissed it as an attempt to gain attention and asked us to take her away. She then revealed the reason for this dramatic scenario, emphasising the consequences of medical negligence by recounting the loss of a patient due to Dr. Naina's absence. Anjali Ma'am, a senior resident, cynically remarked that Dr. Naina should have tried a career in modelling, 'COVID *me bhi video banati thi ye ladki'*. (She even used to make videos during COVID.)

We left for lectures after that and heard the shocking news of Dr. Naina passing away days later. Nobody was ready to explain how it happened. We only got to know about the whole story when Dr. Tanvi mentioned it months later in her blog.

5. 5

Dr. Naina was to meet her fiancé Dr. Aman that Sunday. They chose Sunday because Sundays allowed some leisure time for residents as most of the professors avoided taking rounds on that day. She exchanged her duty with her best friend, Dr. Tanvi who very positively agreed.

Dr. Naina and Dr. Aman, who hadn't seen each other for months, met in the evening. Dr. Naina, challenging the department's norm of wearing traditional attire, dressed in Western clothes. The evening unfolded with the lovebirds reuniting. They welcomed each other with a warm hug, a bear hug actually, after embracing each other for a while Aman kneeled down on one knee and touched her belly, gently rubbing his hands over it.

Aman: 'How's she?'

Naina: 'How do you know that the little one is she?'

Dr. Naina and Dr. Aman had a little beautiful secret. They were expecting a child.

They planned to share this news with their respective families next week. Only one person knew about this and that was her best friend, Dr. Tanvi.

They had a table booked at South Nation café, famous for its delicious South Indian food.

5. 5

Believe me, when they make you work for 18-20 hrs a day, a break starts to feel very strange to you. That day, Naina was excited to meet Aman but also was concerned about her patients. She was every now and then having a check on her phone which, of course, was making Aman annoyed. After all, they were meeting after months.

After a while, he took her phone and put it on silent.

Aman: 'Dac Sahiba, ye hogaya ho apka toh date pe chal le.' (Doctor Ma'am, if you are done with this, can we go on our date now.)

Naina: 'Ya sure, did I tell you about my topic for my thesis?'

Dr. Tanvi had double the workload that Sunday, after attending to her patients she also kept a check on Dr. Naina's patients.

Dr. Tanvi Thapar was known for her calm demeanour and great communication skills with the patients, but that day, her patience was tested. Not only she had to attend to double the patients, but there were 14 admissions in an emergency that Sunday.

She had to deal with everything, and she did. It was already past 1 am now, and she was slumped. Her mind was asking her to take one more round before heading to the bed but her body was not allowing it. She could feel her calf muscles strained. As she reached Dod room (a room where doctors usually take rest), she laid herself on the bed, opening one pair of shoes with the help of her other leg. She could see her knuckles turned purple because of peripheral cyanosis. She had not eaten anything after her breakfast in the morning that too was a cup of coffee and bread toast. She intended to grab something during lunch hours but couldn't because of first, the overwhelming patient load and second, the college canteen stayed closed on Sundays.

Now was her time to rest. Her hunger was dead for now. She lay in perfect anatomical position as if her body had no senses.

Around 3 am, Dr. Tanvi was disturbed from her sleep. Sister Sanjida and Sujata were in Dod, asking her to immediately follow them as one patient was serious. She came back to consciousness and immediately rushed with them to the ward. As she entered the ward, she saw Dr. Mitali Ghosh Ma'am (Head, OBGY) yelling at the sisters. She was asking about the resident on duty.

Her noise had Tanvi scared stiff. She didn't expect her at this time of the day. She thought, 'What brings her here?'

'Who was on duty? If I don't get names, I will make sure you don't get your degrees', said Dr. Ghosh.

After hearing this, Tanvi broke out in a cold sweat.

'Names???,' said Dr. Ghosh.

'Ma'am...I..... Nain...'

'Speak louder. What do you guys get paid for if you can't speak properly?' said Dr.Ghosh.

'Ma'am Naina....Dr. Naina is on duty,' said Dr. Tanvi.

Everybody was shocked, right from third-year residents to nursing staff as they knew it was Dr. Tanvi who had agreed to exchange duty with Dr. Naina that evening.

Around 1 am, midnight, there was a case admitted to the emergency with abdominal pain and a history of vomiting. The patient was known to Dr. Mitali Ghosh. The patient gave a history of missing her periods last month so routine investigations for pregnancy were sent along with ultrasonography. Before final reports were available, the patient passed out due to heavy internal bleeding. The patient had a history of multiple abortions in the past, which made her condition even worse, but all of this information was shared by her family after she passed out.

5. 5

Mitali Ghosh Ma'am, 'I want Dr. Naina in my cabin in five minutes.'

Tanvi tried to contact Naina hundreds of times through calls, WhatsApp, text and even sent her a message on Paytm to pick up her calls.

Failed!!

Tanvi was shaking like a leaf walking from one end corner of the ward to the other. Multiple efforts to contact Dr. Naina failed.

Tanvi tried her best to make stories and get Naina out of this thing, ranging from her being in the washroom to her father being severely ill.

Mitali Ghosh figured out from all the nursing staff that Dr. Naina was not present on her duty that day and she was all steamed up now.

Dr. Mitali Ghosh, 'I will not leave until I confront the killer doctor.'

She was awake waiting in her chamber all night. All junior residents were standing encircling her desk. She had not even once cared to ask them to sit.

It was a perfect Sunday evening for Dr. Naina as she had met her fiancé after months. Aman, last night, showed her the ring he brought for her, for their marriage. It was time to say goodbye, with tears in their eyes and equal excitement to finally get hitched for life in a few months. They headed back to their routine work.

As Dr. Naina was about to enter the ward, Sheela tai who was on duty there immediately stood up. Her eyes were wide open and one hand was covering her mouth, a total bolt from the blue moment for her.

Naina couldn't figure out what just happened. She greeted Sheela tai and moved on. But as she moved through the corridors everybody including the patients now wanted a glimpse of her.

Sujata Sister, 'Ma'am hurry up, the Head ma'am has been waiting for you all night.' There was undoubtedly an element of surprise in this announcement.

'Head Ma'am? Calling me??'

As she moved further, she realised her phone was still on silent mode. Her phone was about to reveal a bombshell for her.

'Naina there is a slight problem.'

'Naina pick up the phone.'

'Naina yaar where on earth are you?'

Hundreds of messages and calls.

The last message was fifteen minutes ago from Tanvi.

'Naina, I am so so sorry. I fucked up.'

(It was then when we final year students were called into Dr. Ghosh Chamber.)

Everybody panicked but Tanvi was in cold sweat. Naina was rushed to the ER in an unconscious state where she regained consciousness after a while.

About twenty minutes had passed after she had gained consciousness and Sujata sister was here with a message from the Head Ma'am.

'Ma'am, Head Ma'am ne bola hai apko bed 15 ka USG karwa ke lane.'

(Ma'am, the Head Ma'am has told you to get a USG scan done for bed no. 15.)

Everybody was shocked. They all were expecting an apology from the Head of the Department for the insult.

Naina: 'Ye....Yes, Sister, I will get it done.' Her voice was still weak but somehow she saw this as a chance to gain back her reputation in front of Hod.

5. 5

Before anyone could make decisions for her, she pulled out a fluid pipe on her own.

'I am fine. It was just because I didn't have food this morning.'

Tanvi: 'Naina, you need to rest. This is not cool. I will get your work done.'

Naina glared towards Tanvi, 'I can do my work. I don't need help from anyone here. I am totally fine.' The last line was only heard by her. She broke down saying this.

She approached the nursing station and asked a sister to take her signatures for DAMA (Discharge against medical advice).

Sister: '*Ma'am apke test hone baki hai.*' (Ma'am, your tests are pending.)

Baad me sister ji! (Later sister!)

On the other hand, Dr. Mitali Ghosh had planned her revenge, which she very politely referred to as a basic training schedule for incompetent residents.

She ordered the head nurse to bring all the files from the store room for the last two years as she needed to evaluate them for mistakes. After spending an hour with the files, she was ready with her plan. She called Dr. Naina to her chamber.

Dr. Naina was scared to death before entering her chamber but she was surprised when was greeted with a smile.

'Come on *Beta*, I have some work for you. As you know we all make mistakes but we all should be given a chance to correct them, right?', said Dr. Ghosh.

Naina: 'Yes....Yes, Ma'am.'

'Great,' said Dr. Ghosh.

'So, I have some file work for you to make you understand ward postings better. All you have to do is to write the summary of patients' progress on a daily basis in each file. Remember it should be written in both *Hindi* and English languages so that it makes your understanding more deeper, will you do it *beta*?'

'Yes, Ma'am. Anything you say, I will, I will.'

She smiled in a conceited manner.

She rang the call bell kept on her desk

Staff: 'Yes Ma'am.'

Take Dr. Naina to the store room, please. She has some work to do.

'And yes Dr. Naina, I advise you to complete the work in two days, otherwise, I will be helpless and have to inform the Medical Negligence Authority of our college to register a complaint in your name for putting an innocent life in danger yesterday.'

Naina's heart skipped a beat. She had to do it anyhow.

'Yes Ma'am, it will be done,' said Dr. Naina.

'It has to be done,' said Dr. Ghosh. I am also getting in touch with your parents to tell them how their daughter made pregnancy excuses to avoid duties.

Naina was shocked. She couldn't believe what she was hearing.

'What Ma'am?', said Naina.

'What? You think you will make excuses and get away,' Dr. Tanvi has explained to me all your excuses. Now get lost,' said Dr. Ghosh.

Naina was steaming. She was ready to go ballistic on Tanvi. She couldn't imagine how her best friend could do this to her. Little did she know that when she was admitted to the ER, during that period, it was Dr. Tanvi who had literally begged in front of Dr. Mitali Ghosh to forgive Naina and give her a chance. Being very emotional she revealed that

5. 5

Naina was pregnant. Dr. Ghosh thought this was a mere gimmick to get her best friend out of trouble.

The situation was bad, but now it was going to be worse when Naina was informed by the head nurse that Ghosh Ma'am had asked her to put counselling notes in *4000* files in two days.

For some time, Naina felt like a dead fish in water. She thought that this was like fighting a losing battle. She regretted everything now, her meeting with Aman, her friendship with Tanvi, and her whole life. But she had to do it, she had to at least try.

Everybody in the ward had strict orders from the Head to not help Dr. Naina in any manner, and those who tried to be smart would be rewarded with the same punishment as her.

For the next two days, Naina didn't sleep and didn't eat. She had to take the bull by the horns.

After two days of extensive hardship, Naina sealed the deal. She submitted the files and asked the head nurse to inform Dr. Mitali Ghosh that her job was done.

The flexor muscles of her hand exhibited fatigue, and her face was swollen. She was not able to extend her digits properly. She was running on empty. She reached her hostel feeling like a zombie. She could sense someone was watching her from the other end of the corridor, 'Tanvi'.

Dr. Tanvi was torn between choices, on one hand, she feared confronting Naina because of the obvious anger she knew she had for her and on the other hand, she wanted to sort out everything with her best friend, and wanted to tell her how communication gap and unfavourable circumstances led to such a mishap.

Naina didn't want to see her face. She opened her door and shut it at lightning speed.

Dr. Naina lay flat on her bed. She had tears in her eyes but had the satisfaction that she saved her degree, saved the dream.

She didn't realise when she went asleep, only to get up with severe pain in her abdomen. Her entire bed sheet was stained with blood, and she immediately rushed to the washroom.

When was I expecting my period? But how can I have my period when I am pregnant?

Soon she realised that she was discharging tissues along with blood from her vagina.

She was shell-shocked. She lost her baby.

Naina was numb. She was not crying. She didn't utter a single word. Her hands and feet were getting cold. The tap which she had opened to wash was not closed. There was water all over which was slowly now entering her living room, sneaking through the lower end of the door.

How was she going to answer her fiancé?

She came back to her living room and started laughing. Yes, you heard it right. She started laughing, but not just normal laughter. This laughter was cynical because she was laughing at herself looking into the mirror for twenty straight minutes. In between, she was pointing in the mirror to herself and saluting with the slogan 'Hey Dr. Naina, the killer' and continued her laughter. She was laughing so hard that after some time, her ribs had started to pain, and her voice was becoming feeble. She wiped her face and whispered, 'Baby, Mumma is coming. Mumma will sort out everything. You are not alone.'

Tanvi decided to end her mental tussle about whether she should go and meet Naina and explain everything to her or not. Somehow she gathered courage and decided to pay

Naina a visit. She locked her room and started to walk towards the other end of the corridor where once her best friend, Naina's room was. As she approached her room, she decided that she should make a call first, 'What if she doesn't want to see me', 'What if I trigger the past she has already suffered'. She tried to call Naina twice but her phone was switched off. Tanvi stood still in the corridor again confused about what she should do, but she knew her best friend. She knew that if she explained what actually happened, she would forgive her. Maybe they would become best friends again. She decided to go to her room and knocked on the door. There was no response. She knocked two more times before she started shouting to introduce herself.

Naina, *mai hu, khol darwaza* (Naina, it's me, open the door.). She knew that Naina would recognise her voice and she didn't need to introduce her name. After all, she was the only friend Naina had and vice versa.

Naina yaar, bas ek bar baat kar le, I need to explain (Naina, just talk to me once, I need to explain). She knocked again... 'Naina, just once yaar.' All her efforts were futile. Naina didn't respond.

5. 5

Tanvi: 'Okay Naina, have your ego. I worked my ass off on your exchange duty when you had fun and now you didn't even care to listen to me. Good, live alone,' she said and banged the door with her fist and started to walk away. As she took a step away from the door, she realised that the door was already open. She just needed to make a push to enter. Tanvi remembered how Naina used to always advise her to not overthink any situation and always communicate whatever she felt. Tanvi was relieved that her best friend was not angry with her. She must be having rest in her room. After all, she was working for the last *48* hours straight. For once, she felt she should leave her to rest and pay her a visit later but she doubted that she could gather courage later to discuss things with her, so she pushed the door. 'Naina, are you ther.....

Dr. Naina Jaiswal had committed suicide. She hanged herself from the ceiling fan. Tanvi was devastated. Aman was devastated. The entire college mourned her death. We had a half day off in honour of her passing.

You must be wondering why I didn't explain what happened to Tanvi, what happened to Aman, Naina's family and all the people associated with Naina after that event, but do you really care?

I mean you do, you do talk about it, share news on your Instagram stories, call the system toxic and then?

Let's be honest, and let's face it. Our politicians consider it normal, while you may see it as a once-in-a while event, but sir/ma'am let me correct you, this is not a once-in-a-while event. The toxicity of a workplace cannot be measured by how many people have committed suicide while working there.

But, it is a part of the training process. If doctors don't work hard, how will they treat patients? Right?

No, it is not the hours of work that make it toxic. It is how you make them work. One resident fears that he might not get signatures for the thesis, whereas the other feels that he might fail even after studying hard just because he said no to his/her senior for some work. We have become so accustomed to learning the harsh way that we now actually don't know the gentle way to learn. Honestly, be it interns or residents, they now believe getting roasted on ward rounds is normal just because it also makes you learn a few points about making a diagnosis. The only hope that carries you from the first year of MBBS life till the end of your medical education is 'I have come so far now, and I can't quit'. But this goes on. Every semester passing by from the first year to the final year gives you mixed feelings. First, it's done, and the second is that more is coming. An added sense of responsibility with each passing year also comes with a fear of facing toxicity, not being able to meet your family, missing your social life, etc.

I don't think Dr. Naina committing suicide and her struggle with Dr. Mitali Ghosh had a direct connection, but surely if you have worked so hard to become a doctor and now feel threatened on a daily basis by the people belonging to your own fraternity, denied food and sleep when you were expecting a baby, insulted in front of your colleagues and juniors, I think all this surely challenges your mental health.

CHAPTER 9

THE FINAL LEAP

5. 5

It was the final week before the results of the final year were going to be announced, and I was panicking like crazy. Natasha told me not to fret about the results. Everyone was getting frustrated because the exam was so tough. But hey, at least I had Natasha by my side. Who knew that studying with someone could make such a difference?

After a week of anticipation, the long-awaited results were finally announced. With great relief, we discovered that all of us had passed our final year exams, except for a few. Fortunately, none of my group members failed. We rejoiced in our success and celebrated as we had finally achieved our dream of becoming doctors. Our hard work and dedication had paid off, and we were ready to start our journey as medical professionals. It was a moment of triumph that we would always cherish.

I went to collect my final year mark sheet from the library. The librarian thought that I was a 1st-year student and started making fun of me, '*Kharach tumhi final year pass kela na. Aapko dadhi kyu nahi aayi abhi tak ?*' (You passed final year exams and still have no beard on your face). I ignored this awkward conversation, smiled, took my final year mark sheet and left.

We were anxiously awaiting the release of our internship roster on the notice board. After it was finally posted, I realised with a mix of excitement and trepidation that I had been assigned to the Department of Paediatrics as my first rotation. It felt like diving straight into the deep end, tackling one of the toughest departments right off the bat.

On my first day of posting, I saw interns in different colour scrubs. The way they were dressed was incongruous, ranging from emerald to forest green, some even in blue or maroon scrubs, and some like me preferred to watch other people for a few days and observe the best colour scrub that would suit my body. Together we looked like Power Rangers.

Sessions with Dr. Dhawan made me realise that I also needed to keep my passion alive if I wanted to cope with the lifelong study schedule. So I decided that I would watch a movie specific to each department before starting my postings there. After doing some research, and consulting with friends I came up with the following list:

5. 5

1. Medicine – Patch Adams
2. Surgery – Something the Lord Made
3. OBGY – Revolutionary Road
4. Paediatrics – Extraordinary Measures
5. Community Medicine – Contagion
6. Psychiatry – A Beautiful Mind
7. Radiology – The Lighthouse
8. Anaesthesia – Awake
9. Orthopaedics – Bone Collector
10. Ophthalmology – At First Sight
11. ENT – Sound of Metal
12. Casualty – Code Black

I realised that the paediatric posting was not only tough for us but also for the parents of the toddlers. I could see mothers sitting and sleeping in that little area around the cradle of the baby, having no idea about when they were going to have their next meal, trying to feed their babies, upset about their prognosis, feeling helpless when we prick their child time and again for cannulation. In Paediatrics, I realised what true love is, and what actually courage is.

Parents who couldn't even afford to buy two-time meals for themselves were keen to provide their baby with the best of facilities. However, there was also a sense of relief knowing that once I conquered Paediatrics, no other posting would seem quite as challenging. Paediatrics had been my favourite subject during my final year, and I had initially decided to pursue a career in child healthcare. Yet, after just twenty-one days in the department, I came to the realisation that it might not be the right path for me. The workload, combined with the delicate nature of caring for children, required an immense amount of patience and vigilance. Unlike adult patients, neonates couldn't articulate their complaints, making diagnosis and treatment even more challenging. Our second rotation integrated with Paediatrics was in the Department of Forensic Medicine and Toxicology. The walls were adorned with posters raising awareness about drug abuse, dowry deaths, and suicide prevention. As we walked through the department, the sight of bones used for identification purposes triggered flashbacks to our anatomy classes, serving as a stark reminder of the grim realities of forensic work. Following that, we were assigned to elective

5. 5

rotations, spending two weeks each in Radiology and the TB & Chest Department. After the demanding Paediatrics rotation, these weeks felt akin to a honeymoon period. Without night shifts, we typically wrapped up our duties by five in the evening. Next on the roster was the General Medicine rotation, which proved to be slightly less taxing than Paediatrics. However, the workload remained substantial, with interns tasked with duties such as blood pressure monitoring in the OPD and accompanying faculty on rounds. Each faculty member had their own distinct approach to patient care, and adapting to their routines added an extra layer of complexity to our responsibilities. As I reflected on my experiences of two months as an intern, certain insights became evident. Firstly, there was a pressing need for colleges to prioritise training interns in life-saving procedures rather than burdening them with administrative tasks. Additionally, the quality of the internship experience hinged greatly on the calibre of our seniors (PGs). Supportive and knowledgeable seniors facilitated our learning and growth, whereas toxic individuals only sought to offload their workload onto us.

Our brief stint in the Department of Psychiatry proved to be eye-opening. Building trust with patients was paramount, as they needed to feel safe and understood in order to open up about their struggles. Beyond the clinical setting, psychiatry had the potential to reshape one's outlook on life, emphasising the importance of patience and non-judgmental support in the healing process. It was my second day in the psychiatry ward. The first patient I met was a young boy who was struggling with OCD. He was convinced that he had cancer because of a small swelling on his cheek, and his anxiety was overwhelming. He had even endured multiple COVID infections during the pandemic, each time leading to weeks of isolation. He felt as though he was cursed with bad luck and couldn't focus on his studies due to the fear of his own mortality. It was a poignant reminder that life can be profoundly unfair, and some individuals bear more than their share of hardship.

During my week in the Neurosurgery department, I faced difficult challenges. I had to calculate GCS scores and review MRI reports for interpretation, which proved to be quite daunting. I sought written reports to ensure I provided the best care possible. I encountered a patient's attendant who revealed that his wife hadn't spoken in six months. His words, 'and if she speaks then there is no sorrow in my life,' resonated with me deeply. It reminded me of the uncertainty and hardships that many face, often unexpectedly and with no clear resolution.

I spent seven weeks in the Department of Surgery followed by two weeks in the Department of Anaesthesia. Both departments were incredibly rewarding experiences. Initially, I grappled with shaky hands while assisting in surgeries, but I soon realised that success in surgery requires meticulous preparation. It's about attention to detail. It's about you getting disciplined, getting adequate sleep and nutrition to sustain through long hours, and thoroughly reviewing the procedures you're about to assist in. We all eagerly commemorated our first suture with photographs. For those who fear making mistakes in surgery, it's essential not to let that fear consume you. Mistakes are inevitable, and proficiency comes with practice and persistence. Don't hesitate to seek out opportunities for growth.

My posting in surgery OT was complex. No, it wasn't like I was there to make decisions on where to make an incision or what to do when you find a tumour when you operate on a lump. My postings were complex because I had no idea what my job was. It felt like I was qualified enough to be in that room but not qualified enough to do anything. I realised there is a gap between theory and practice, a long wait. So I surrendered to the thought that maybe this was the time for me to learn not by doing, but by my senses— observing how the lead surgeon holds his knife and maintains his focus. I began to realise that maybe anaesthesia is a far cooler job than being a surgeon. I was told to counsel my patients before surgery. I thought explaining to them the duration and possible complications could be enough, but they wanted to know more. One old guy before his hernia surgery had asked me what I would be doing with his body. He wanted to know the steps of the surgery. I was much relieved that this was a case of open hernia surgery. The same case I had in my final year of university viva. I explained to him that how after making an incision over the weakened area of the abdominal wall, we would expose the hernia site and repair the weak spot, and after that we would have closure. I told him not to worry, '*Mee sarvakahi sambhaalun ghein.*' (I will take care of everything.)

I escorted him to the OT room, got washed and stood right next to him as the anaesthesia guys were trying to sedate him. The seniors entered the OT and told me that I had only one job today. As he was a hypertensive patient, I had to keep my eyes on the monitor all the time. Before turning my head towards the monitor, I looked at the patient for one last time. His eyes were affixed at me. If eyes could speak and if I could hear his mind, he was saying, 'You son of a.......You are no doc .'

After the operation was over, we were told to submit samples for test in the pathology lab and after that, we all friends used to meet for lunch.

Yash got a text from his mom saying, '*Beta*, are you in the OT?' Frustrated, he put his phone back in his bag. He told us, 'The only constant throughout the years has been my mom ranting about my grandmother.' We consoled him by saying, 'One more constant is our friendship throughout college life.'

5.5

We finished our evening rounds, took notes, and reported to our seniors. Then we decided to grab some snacks at the canteen. Yash took his phone out of his bag and was surprised to see a dozen missed calls from his family members and a voice note from his mom. Considering this might be a serious situation, we all decided to listen to it together. In the voice note, his mom was blabbering like a child, 'Dadi passed away in her sleep today, *beta*. How can she leave us? How can God do this to us?'

We could see Yash getting teary-eyed, but this is where men often struggle—they don't know how to express their emotions. We all just sat together in the canteen without speaking a word for the next thirty minutes. Somehow, it felt like a personal loss to all of us. Listening to the funny banter between his mom and Dadi had always given us joy. Finally, Yash decided to break the silence, 'Jai, Zeeshan, I love you guys. I know this sounds absurd right now, but I realised we should say this more often to our loved ones. Dadi will never know that Mom thinks well about her. Mom could never now say it to her.'

5. 5

In the realm of anaesthesia, our rotations included stints in the ICU, a place where one can acquire a myriad of skills—from arterial blood gas sampling to central venous line procedures. The challenge, however, lay in the night shifts. Unlike in medicine or surgery, where brief coffee breaks are feasible, the ICU demands unwavering vigilance. Patients' vital signs can fluctuate rapidly, necessitating a cohesive team effort where every member's contribution is invaluable.

Transitioning to the Department of Obstetrics & Gynaecology, we found ourselves amidst a whirlwind of drama and frustration. We sorely missed Dr. Naina, whose presence could have potentially altered the dynamic. Despite the challenges, the Head of Department, Mitali Ghosh persistently painted Dr. Naina as incompetent and unfit—a sentiment echoed throughout our tenure.

Our journey then led us to the Department of Community Medicine, where we split our time between rural and urban centres. Taking charge of the OPD initially felt daunting, accustomed as we were to work under seniors' guidance. Yet, with perseverance, we managed well. It was here that the stark reality of healthcare inequality struck me. Poverty emerged as the primary obstacle to good health, emphasising the need not only for free medication but also for comprehensive health education. Our daily field visits, though initially dreaded, evolved into cherished interactions with village residents. Despite the occasional theatrics surrounding medication shortages, the warmth and respect shown by the villagers fostered a deep appreciation for our profession. Snacking at local shops and the simplicity of village life underscored the importance of gratitude and perspective.

We got the news that the local quacks had bilked thousands from villagers in the name of treatment. We tried to confront the village sarpanch regarding this but his boorish behaviour at the health camp offended everyone. We got to know that he himself received a commission to let this practice continue. The quack's chicanery was exposed during our investigation. He was prescribing antibiotics for mild cases of dengue which was creating antibody-mediated resistance amongst the villagers. What the quack deserved was defenestration, but we could not do anything, as local officials were involved. Eliminating dengue cases from the village was tough. Initially, our desultory conversations caused delays, and then later for the first time, we realised how the levels of prevention we learned in our third year had to come into action. We started with educating the community about how dengue is transmitted and methods of its prevention. Next was to introduce natural predators like guppy fish (*Poecilia reticulata)* to eat mosquito larvae in water bodies. We advised villagers to wear long-sleeved clothing and use mosquito repellents. Other measures included installing mosquito nets or screens on windows and doors. The use of approved dengue vaccines like Dengvaxia was also recommended.

The coffee we used to have at PHC (Primary Health Centre) lacked flavour and aroma, so I decided to carry my own coffee to the centre. Jlo opined that this was the best coffee I had made so far. The department staff who used to accompany us to the centre had a very furtive personality, he was friendly with us at the centre but used to complain to the Head behind our back. Some villagers passed gauche remarks when asked about their complaints that used to embarrass everyone. Jlo's hedonistic personality worried everyone at the centre. She considered the posting as holidays, made some friends in the village and used to have her *Chai-Nashta* sessions with them on a daily basis. Her imperious tone made everyone resent her, especially other girls in the group. But Jlo was unwilling to compromise. Our college authority was generous towards the villagers so they decided to build a 25-bed hospital near the panchayat area of the village. The panchayat, of course, refused any cooperation as there was no commission involved.

While being posted in the village I realised that there was no panacea for all of life's problems. You have to deal with individual issues at different times throughout your life.

Subhramanyam, as usual, was a restive personality, whether it was the question of who would get a window seat on a bus or who would eat the most number of *kachoris*. He considered everything a competition.

The most impactful experience of being a medical student was during my posting in the Casualty department. A number of cases I encountered there will stay with me for years to come. Although the staff in the ER were often boorish, the residents ensured that we made the most of our two-week rotation. Unlike other departments, where we would spend time idly loitering, in the ER we were actively learning by doing. We observed cases first-hand and gained knowledge from the real-life experiences of our seniors, rather than solely relying on textbooks. At times, the ER felt chaotic, with attendants crowding the counters and incessantly making inquiries. However, we learned to tune out the noise and stay focused on our work.

It was a cold evening just before New Year's Eve when I was posted in the emergency department. It had been a quiet shift except for a few minor cases. My shift was about to end at eight and then we heard the sound of a siren from outside the emergency complex. I rushed to attend to the case, and there I saw paramedics unloading the patient onto the stretcher. They quickly briefed me about the case. The patient was a young male in his twenties, with multiple contusions and abrasions and a possible shoulder dislocation. He was unconscious, and his body turned pale. We quickly connected him with the monitor and found his vitals to be unstable. His GCS score was even very low. I started the head-to-toe examination and asked nurses to inform seniors and secure an IV line. A CT scan was ordered by Dr. Kanodia, who was the attending surgeon for the night. The patient's airway was managed by a team of anaesthetics. Everyone around the patient was in a panic state except for Dr. Kanodia, which made it easy for him to make decisions. The CT scan was performed, and we found a large contusion in the frontal lobe. Also, there was a rib fracture found on the chest CT. Dr. Kanodia declared that we needed to operate the patient. The patient was prepped for surgery and was taken to the OT under the observation of anaesthetists. Dr. Kanodia asked me to scrub in. I was excited because this was going to be my first trauma surgery case. I was taking mental notes about the procedures happening step-by-step. I wished to participate but I somehow knew that this was not the place where I could make mistakes and then correct them. Here any small mistake could take a young person's life. But Dr. Kanodia saw my willingness to participate and offered me the last skin suture. By the time surgery concluded it was already 1 am. The patient had stable vitals now and was being shifted to the ICU. There we needed to monitor him for any signs of sepsis, assess his GCS scores and ensure that the fracture was healing properly. His journey to recovery would be long, probably he was never going to be the same but at least he was alive, and at least we could save a life. That day what I learned from Dr. Kanodia was to maintain our composure when faced with difficult situations, if he had wasted time panicking then we could have lost a life. After saving a dozen snaps from the OT, I finally handed over my duty to a night intern.

I and my friends along with Natasha decided that we needed a vacation. So we decided to go to Goa, but wait this is not our '*Dil Chahta hai*' moment. To go to Goa, you need money and should ensure your bookings are made. Natasha suggested we should go to a hill station like Shimla, but I had heard there was a blizzard in Shimla that winter.

So, after the plans for Goa, Shimla, and Manali fell through, we thought, 'Why not head to Delhi instead?' I have always believed that Delhi has a soul. My physiology professor once told me that my vital capacity was impressive, so despite Delhi's pollution, I barely felt it. During cab rides, I often preferred open windows and loud music—the kind you play only when you're with friends, usually the 90s hit list. We even visited some old tannery shops in Old Delhi. Another unique characteristic of Delhi was its blend of people from different cultures across India. Whether it was late-night parties at social or our cosy picnic at Lodhi Gardens, we enjoyed every bit of it. This was my first or maybe also the last trip of college life with Natasha.

Believe me when I say this—you can't be truly fair to someone if it's their first love and not yours. Falling in love for the second time feels different. You don't want to get hurt again. You want her to be flawless, forgetting that we are all human, and we all have flaws. You don't get anxious when she doesn't call, nor are you desperate to resolve things immediately after a fight. In fact, you don't take it too seriously. You assume it's normal, and time will heal it. But for someone experiencing love for the first time, this can be hard to understand. You start prioritising sleep. You focus on your own preferences, even in your playlist. You balance time between friends and your relationship, remembering to call your mom and keeping track of your GT scores. Natasha already had low expectations, but I didn't think that I was ready to do anything that wasn't authentic to me. I wasn't the same Jai anymore. I didn't pretend that I didn't smoke cigarettes, I didn't mark the first day we kissed, and I didn't bother cleaning my room before she visited. I had no idea whether this was normal or not. Does falling in love mean being overexcited all the time, or does it mean becoming more practical? I always thought practical people couldn't be good lovers, yet here I was, turning into one of them.

Back at my postings, one incident deeply affected me—the death of a ten-year-old in the casualty ward. I had performed the intubation successfully, but the lingering thought that I might have caused this disaster tormented me. I shared this with Natasha, and she tried her best to console me. It worked but only for a while. I felt like everyone who passed by was staring at me, their eyes accusing me, their body language shifting when I was around. None of this was true, of course, but it took me a week to accept that.

My perspective changed after I met Dr. Dhawan. He told me that my reaction was very normal, especially after losing a young patient, but getting disturbed showed how much I care. He said, 'This was your strength, not your weakness.

5. 5

No matter how skilled you were, some outcomes were just out of our control. Every experience, no matter how painful, was eventually going to make you a better doctor. When you share this experience with other fellow medicos, you will realise you are not alone. We all have gone through this phase. As a doctor, it's your responsibility to give every patient the best chance. Treat yourself with the kindness you would offer a colleague in the same situation.'
Casualty posting was also a place where you find unusual and funny cases. I encountered a sixteen-year-old boy visiting at 3 am in the night because he was getting palpitations as his girlfriend had blocked him. I said to him, '*Beta, abhi toh tere polio drops khatam hue hi, kahaan tu itna soch raha hai.*' But he insisted that I should admit him, so I decided to refer him to the psychiatry ward. When he visited the ward, he saw the patients there— somebody playing table tennis alone, somebody having imaginary tea with Shakespeare, and many more. The boy went back home in thirty minutes.

The workload in casualty was directly proportional to the number of patients admitted. Luckily this Sunday evening, the patient load was low. My job was to inform the surgery resident regarding an RTA case admitted some time ago. A brother there told me that new residents had joined and their numbers were available in the casualty register. I asked him, 'Why don't you tell me the number from the register and I will make a call', with a stern look he agreed. So I called the resident, 'Hello Sir, I am Jai, an intern posted here in casualty. We have a new case. The patient has a history of RTA with a GCS of E2V4M4. Kindly visit and examine the case.'

So, whatever I had to say, I said in one go, without bothering to listen from the other end. What I could only hear was a 'Hmm, okay......' from the other end of the call, and to my surprise, there was a female resident on call. I wish I could have made my first impression not so bad. Meanwhile, I decided to visit the patient, after all, till the resident arrived I was the *Bade dac* Sahab here. I was assuring the patient party that this was no problem.

'We handle hundreds of such cases every day.' I had no idea that the resident on call was here, and she was standing beside me. After some time, the brother pointed out that Ma'am is here, Sir. So the thing is when you have few days left in your internship and new residents join, you don't see them with much respect. You are like I have studied in this college for years and you have just arrived, so you better respect me, okay? So, I continued my lecture on subdural hematoma to the patient party. I wanted to include the newly joined resident in my lecture, in case she could benefit from it. So I turned back...........umm, maybe I shouldn't have turned back, like never ever. What are the worst things that can happen to me? I felt nothing could be worse than this, nothing even comes close. She said, 'Why did you stop?' Please continue Dr. Jai Verma. She still takes my full name when she is disappointed in my actions. It was Dr. Afreen Sheikh, Junior Resident, Department of General Surgery.

No, this world can't be so small. Life can't run in circles, and you can't have your ex at your workplace. How could I have dared to break this beautiful person's heart? She was so perfect, and we were so much in love. It was like time froze. I froze. Here in front of me was someone with whom I had spent countless nights walking around the campus, talking about everything and nothing at all. Her presence was like a thunderstorm on a bright sunny day. For a moment, I didn't know whether to run towards her or pretend like I hadn't seen her at all.

Afreen said, 'Lucky for you that I have been assigned casualty posting for this week.' The busy schedule of ER didn't leave the room for small talk or an awkward pause.

After the shift was over, Afreen asked me, 'So, how have you been?'

The truth was I hadn't been doing great. The breakup had hit me hard, and it had taken time to recover from the way things ended. But with her standing in front of me again, I couldn't complain.

I said, 'I have been okay.'

She said, 'You are doing well, Jai. I can see you care about patients. We should catch up sometime when we are not working.'

Afreen's return made me realise that life was full of strange coincidences.

5. 5

The only couple who survived for 5. 5 years were Zeeshan and Jlo. They had reached a stage of relationship while in college that when you saw them apart, you would still assume they were in a relationship, unlike other couples at the beginning of college life, who when spotted separately, would make people speculate that had broken up. I could still read the conversation on the back of my notebook I had with Zeeshan when he and Jlo had just started dating. 'Nobody who truly loves does reasonable shit, Jai'. I could still read it because I had been using the same notebook for 5. 5 years. I called it my unofficial 20th notebook. It had Erb's palsy written somewhere, somewhere there was cephalosporin's classification, somewhere you could find about the layers of the retina. Subsequent rotations in Ophthalmology and ENT provided diverse perspectives. Ophthalmology, with its blend of surgical and medical aspects, offered a well-rounded experience. Conversely, ENT proved less appealing, with the intricate complexities of the ear canal resembling a labyrinth. In orthopaedics, a sense of authority permeated the atmosphere, bolstering my confidence and honing my dressing skills.

5. 5

Natasha had an unstinted support towards her loved ones. She was here for my birthday. Natasha brought with her a cake. I was surprised to know that she had baked this cake by herself. The cake had an ambrosial taste. When somebody bakes a cake for you, it feels special. I also remember meeting Dr. Dhawan that day who looked debonnaire in his suit. I was amazed that he remembered my birthday. Dr. Dhawan always dressed in a modish way. What was unusual with him recently was that he was not attending cases after Dr. Naina's demise.

I cajoled my internship group that day to join the celebrations, as this would be my last birthday to celebrate in college. We treated the table in the Dod as a timbrel for giving a background score to Jlo's voice. Natasha even bought a hat for my birthday which honestly made me look like a masquerader. Natasha's foibles were desserts, and she, on her own, ate half the cake. I personally hated the fondant over the cake so I preferred the base, the not-so-creamy layer. The only soothing thing after tedious duty hours was the euphonious voice of Natasha. We used to have lunch almost every day together. Natasha, like Afreen, was garrulous but she also had a calm and peaceful vibe.

5. 5

Natasha and I planned to move to Delhi after our internship to prepare for the PG entrance test together.

I met Aadarsh in his room before leaving the college. He was enjoying his coffee, with books scattered all around. When I first met him in the second year, I thought he had a taciturn nature. For people who don't know him, he still comes across that way even today.

In his room, he was giving me suggestions on books to read next. That was when the idea came to my mind, and I asked him, 'Do you think we should write a book?'

'A book?', he said.

'Yes, about our college life,' I replied.

'Okay. So, you finally agree that we should let people know our perspectives,' he said.

'Ya, maybe it's a good time now,' I said.

'Okay,' he said.

I hadn't expected him to agree so easily. Neither of us had any idea of how to write a book—all we had was our experiences and the way we had perceived college life. Two very different perspectives were ready to intertwine. Let's see how it goes.

Signs were to be taken from Heads of all Departments at the completion of our internship. Case papers were to be submitted for signatures. I repeatedly went to the HOD for signatures, but they postponed it even if the person was five minutes late and asked the intern to come back later.

In the end, I want to say that you are not alone in this struggle. The pressure is not a reflection of your ability, nor is it an indication that you are not capable. In fact, what you are feeling is simply a reflection of how important this task is. The syllabus is your guide, not an obstacle. You may find yourself in environments where there is little room for failure. It's easy to get caught up in the rat race for best scores and to expect admiration from your professors and peers, but what you need to keep in mind is that the goal is to become a compassionate and skilled physician, not just to emerge as the top scorer. You all are the future of healthcare and you have the power to shape the culture of medicine in the years to come. The lack of immediate recognition does not diminish your value or the importance of what you are doing. The real rewards come in the quiet moments when a patient thanks you for your care. Lean on each other, share your struggles and seek help when you need it. Your journey is hard, but it is one of immense value.

A voice echoes from the stage, steady and clear 'Jai'.

For a moment, I didn't react. I had been so lost in the tide of memories. In some time, it hit me. This is not a memory, this is now. The moment that once felt so distant is finally here. My fingers grasp the certificate. I finally took a deep breath.

And just like that, the story ends where it began.

5. 5

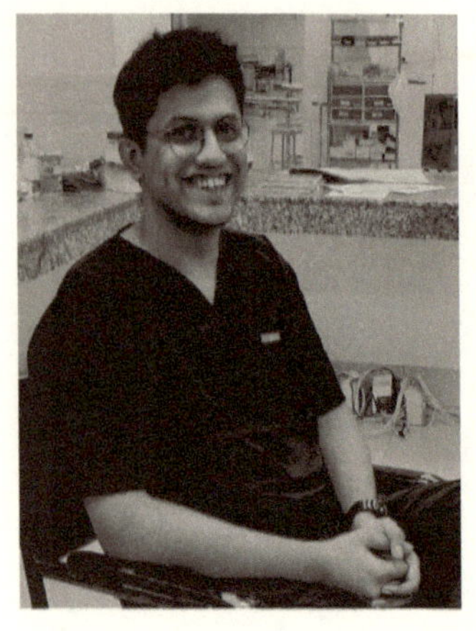

Dr. Jaising Verma That joke you made on my name was very funny. Brand ambassador of Jai Singchanna. He did his MBBS from VPMC.He is currently a resident in MD Anesthesia. He was a child artist in a hindi feature film "Bajra vs. Burger" and cinema has not left him since. He also has dimples for no reasons and wear spectacles which make him look like a muggle harry potter.

Dr. Aadarsh Shivum
is an MBBS graduate
with a deep love for
books and coffee.
Passionate about
blending storytelling
with medicine, he aims
to inspire others
through his writing and
unique perspective on
life, healing and the
human experience.

www.ingramcontent.com/pod-product-compliance
Lightning Source LLC
Chambersburg PA
CBHW031128130726
47988CB00006B/2275